Discard

THE BIRTHDAY ROOM

KEVIN HENKES

A GREENWILLOW BOOK

HarperTrophy®
An Imprint of HarperCollinsPublishers

The Birthday Room
Copyright © 1999 by Kevin Henkes
All rights reserved. No part of this book may be used or reproduced in any
manner whatsoever without written permission except in the case of brief
quotations embodied in critical articles and reviews. Printed in the United States
of America. For information address HarperCollins Children's Books, a division of
HarperCollins Publishers,
1350 Avenue of the Americas, New York, NY 10019.

Library of Congress Cataloging-in-Publication Data
Henkes, Kevin.
   The birthday room / Kevin Henkes.
      p.   cm.
   "Greenwillow Books."
   Summary: When twelve-year-old Ben visits his uncle in Oregon, he feels
caught in the strained relationship between his mother and her brother while he
also begins to accept himself as an artist.
   ISBN 0-688-16733-0 — ISBN 0-06-443828-7 (pbk.)
   [1. Family life—Fiction.   2. Uncles—Fiction.   3. Self-acceptance—Fiction.]
I. Title.
PZ7.H389B1   1999   98-39887
[Fic]—dc21   CIP
                                                                        AC

First Harper Trophy edition, 2001
Visit us on the World Wide Web!
www.harperchildrens.com

FOR LAURA, WILL, CLARA, AND SUSAN

Contents

Part One

HERE

1

TWO OF THE THINGS Benjamin Hunter received for his twelfth birthday took him completely by surprise: a room and a letter. The room was from his parents. The letter was from his uncle.

The room was on the second floor of the house, in the tree-shaded corner of what until a few months earlier had been a musty, unused attic. Ben's parents had reclaimed the attic by having it remodeled to add extra living space to their small, cramped bungalow. Two dormers had been raised—one on the front and one on the back of the house—and three rooms had been built. The largest room was for Ben's mother to use as a weaving studio. The other good-size room was for Ben's father; he had been dreaming for years of a quiet space all his own where he could work on his poetry and listen to his jazz CDs. And the third room, long and low roofed, had been planned as a reading room with a comfortable overstuffed chair, a skylight, and plenty of shelves to accommodate the overflow of books that seemed to multiply in stacks all over the house, starting in corners and spreading to end tables, countertops, and ottomans like some persistent growth.

Ben had watched the progress of the renovation with great interest. Seeing the exposed structure of the house fascinated him——the beams and wires, the ancient plaster and lath stripes. The crew working on the house, he thought, wasn't unlike a surgical team performing an operation. At the height of the project, the house was a body, skin peeled back to reveal muscles, bones, veins, arteries, and organs.

When the work was completed, the reading room seemed to have been forgotten. The shelves and chair never materialized. Ben just assumed that his parents were both so consumed with setting up their own private rooms that the reading room was temporarily abandoned. They would get around to it eventually, but obviously it wasn't a priority.

Soon thereafter, on his twelfth birthday, when Ben's parents coaxed him from bed before dawn and led him upstairs, the door to the reading room was bound in stiff, blue velvet ribbon. The bow in the center was as big and round as a basketball.

"Happy birthday," said his mother as she straightened a curled length of ribbon hanging down from the bow. Her voice was mild, with a trace of first-thing-in-the-morning hoarseness. Her eyes moved from Ben to the ribbon and back, and she smiled with parted lips.

"All yours, bud," said his father. He opened the door, and without looking, reached around the jamb and flipped on the switch for the overhead light. He nodded, inviting Ben to enter.

Ben stepped into the room. His eyes tightened against the brightness. The room was empty. "I don't get it," he replied.

"The *room*—it's yours," his mother explained. "An art studio."

"What about the reading room?" Ben asked.

"Forget the reading room," said his father. "You're an artist. You need a place to work." He went past Ben to the opposite side of the room to look out the skylight. There was nothing to see but darkness.

"We'll get you an easel or a drawing table," his mother told him. "Whatever you need."

"Wow," Ben said, faking enthusiasm. He blinked. "Thank you."

His mother had been standing on the threshold. When she walked into the room, the pocket of her thin bathrobe caught on the doorknob. The door was pulled along behind her until it was only open a crack. "If you could paint *Yellow Sky* among all the clutter on the kitchen table," she said, readjusting her robe, "just think what you can do here." She nudged the door wide open again.

Ben nodded. He could tell how pleased his parents were with the gift. Because he was a lark and his parents were owls, he knew that they had made a great effort to rise early to present their gift before he had

had the chance to wake and discover the decorated door on his own.

"Wow," Ben said again. He didn't want to disappoint them. He loved his parents more than he could say. "Great. This is so great."

The room smelled new, of fresh paint. Glossy white beadboard covered the walls. The look and feel was like that of the inside of a cottage.

His mother kissed his cheek and his father kissed the top of his head, and they both hugged him at the same time, encircling him with their arms, making what they used to call a "Ben sandwich," but because he was thinking of *Yellow Sky* and the empty room and what it meant, he barely felt the embrace. He kissed the air twice, once for each of his parents, which was the closest he'd gotten to actually kissing them in months.

Ben's father yawned noisily like a lazy dog. "I desperately need coffee. And you," he said, facing his son as they broke away from one another, "you need your birthday breakfast. Twelve. I can hardly believe it."

Ben could hardly believe it either. But, whereas his father couldn't believe how quickly the last twelve years had spun by, Ben couldn't believe how long it had taken to turn twelve. In another slow year, he'd finally be a teenager.

Downstairs, in the kitchen, Ben blew out twelve candles stuck into a stack of blueberry pancakes. His parents sang to him and toasted him with orange juice. The three of them ate, while out the window the birds awakened, then chattered and called from the heavy branches nearby and beyond.

When he had finished eating, Ben made stripes on his plate by dragging his fork through the remaining maple syrup. He drew a rectangle. A door. His door. In the seconds before the birthday-room door had been opened, Ben had shivered, one small shiver of excitement. The prospect of what wonderful thing or things could be concealed behind the closed door had made his mind race, guessing. It had to be something too large to put in a regular box and wrap in a normal way. A new bicycle? A big-screen TV? A CD player with giant speakers? A year's supply of cream soda? When he had fully realized what the gift was—and wasn't—his excitement vanished as quickly as the flames on his birthday candles had when he blew at them.

Now swirls and wavy rows like a plowed field completely decorated Ben's plate. He laid the fork down diagonally across the pattern. Little beads of syrup shone on the tines.

"A masterpiece," his mother said lightly, leaning over the table, eyeing the design on the plate. She winked.

"*Composition with Fork and Syrup* by Benjamin Hunter," said his father. "He's a genius. He doesn't even need a pencil, a brush, or canvas. Just give him a fork and a dirty dish and let him loose."

"You guys," said Ben, a bit embarrassed.

"When interviewed," his father continued in a deep, mock-reporter's voice, "his parents, Edward Hunter and Julie Benjamin, admitted to being so proud of him they feared they might burst."

"Daaad."

Ben's mother raised her hand to her neck. The edges of her nails were rough. After clearing her throat, she asked, "Do you really like it? Is it the world's best gift, or a dud?" Her look was penetrating, as if she were trying to read tiny print inside his head.

"World's best," Ben lied.

"Really?"

"Yes." Ben smiled, a crooked smile, and dropped his gaze. Absently, he opened his hands and flexed his nine fingers. He composed his face. "It was such a big surprise. Maybe I'm kind of in shock, or something. It's a big thing to get a whole room."

Ben's father chuckled.

Soon the table—the end where they had eaten, the end that was not hidden by books, newspapers, pens, postage stamps, recipe cards, laundry—was cleared and wiped, the dishes stacked in the sink. As they left the kitchen to shower and get ready for the day, Ben's father said, "So, big guy, do you feel different? Changed?"

"Hmm," Ben breathed. "Not really." He swallowed. "Not at all." But that wasn't exactly true.

He followed his parents down the dim narrow hallway that divided the house. He turned into his bedroom, then turned back abruptly. I lied, he thought, steadily watching his parents walk away. I lied to you today.

≈   ≈

Later the same morning, the letter arrived. Ben's parents were at work. They owned a store called Just Books on State Street near campus, where they sold exactly that—just books. No coffee, no magazines, no newspapers. Because it was summertime, July, Ben usually went to the store to help or to simply hang out. He had grown up at the store, as had several of his friends. On this particular morning, Ben had lagged behind at home, waiting for the mail to see if his grandmother, Lucy, had come through with her customary birthday gift—a crisp two-dollar bill for each year of his life.

Gramma Lu was Ben's one and only living grandparent, his father's mother. She was a resident in a nursing home in northern Wisconsin, a five-hour drive from Madison, where Ben lived. Gramma Lu had diabetes. Three years earlier, her right foot had been amputated due to complications of the disease. Since then, Ben had felt connected to her in a new, strange way.

When he had seen her footless leg for the first time, he was wide eyed, but not frightened at all. Usually, though, there was nothing out of the ordinary to see during their visits; Gramma Lu always covered her legs completely with a tightly knit, unusually long, mint green afghan she'd made herself that collected on the floor in a bulky heap, hiding everything.

The mail came. The money from Gramma Lu was there, wrapped in a plain sheet of paper marked with a big shaky *X* and a small misshapen *O*, nothing else. The paper, the twelve bills, and the pale yellow envelope smelled strongly of lilacs—her perfume.

Ben liked receiving the two-dollar bills because they seemed rare and notable, and worth so much more than their face value. Each year he saved at least one in the dilapidated leather pouch he kept in the back of his sock drawer.

Ben counted the money twice, then flipped through the other pieces of mail. There were catalogs, a magazine, advertisements for stores, and a business envelope he nearly missed.

The envelope was addressed to Mr. Benjamin Hunter. The postmark read Eugene, Oregon. The return address on the back confirmed what Ben had somehow already guessed—the envelope was from his uncle, Ian. Just holding the envelope made Ben's knees go hollow. He wanted to open it, and he didn't want to open it. He wanted his parents there with him, and yet he was grateful to be alone.

Minutes passed. The electric clock in the kitchen hummed. The screen door shifted on its hinges in a slight breeze. A cat screeched somewhere outside, somewhere close. And then there was the sound of the envelope being ripped open.

Dear Benjamin,

I've rewritten this letter too many times to mention, trying to get it exactly right. Even if I didn't do that—get it exactly right—I hope I got it right enough.

First off—happy birthday! Twelve is certainly a big deal. I can only imagine how you've grown since I last saw you. You were really only a baby then, and I called you Benjy.

I'm sure it's a surprise to receive this letter out of the blue. I don't know how much you know about me, how much your mother has told you. But that doesn't really matter. For now, I'd just like to extend an invitation for you to visit before school begins again in the fall. The invitation is extended to your parents as well, of course. I live in the country near Eugene, Oregon. I think you'd all enjoy it out here—the hills are golden this time of year and I'm surrounded by orchards. A bonus—an escape from the Wisconsin humidity and mosquitoes.

I'll call in a week or so to discuss details after you've all had a chance to think about and talk about my invitation. Too much time has passed, and I want to change that. I want to see you and know you again.

> Sincerely,
> Uncle Ian

P.S. I will pay for the plane tickets.

Ben replaced the letter in the envelope, folded the envelope in half, and shoved it into his back pants pocket. Then he rode his bicycle to his parents' store as fast as he could. He pedaled relentlessly, unaware of the muggy air, or traffic, or the sounds of the city. At one point, he nearly collided with a small dog on a long leash. The dog's yelps and its owner's warnings seemed to be filtered through layers of cotton, separate from his world. In that moment, he felt as though his world were breaking open, and that twelve would be an adventure.

2

WHEN BENJAMIN HUNTER was two and a half years old, the little finger on his left hand was cut off in an accident. The accident happened while his uncle was baby-sitting him. They were in his uncle's basement workshop. His uncle had dropped out of college, traveled for a couple of years, and had been teaching himself how to build furniture. On that bleak January day, his uncle was finishing a chair for Ben.

Perhaps it was foolish to have Ben in the workshop, but the legs on the chair were several inches too long and his uncle wanted to make the chair perfect and he didn't want to wait because he was excited about it and so was Ben, who jumped up and down like a toy and shouted: "I like my chair! I want my chair!" Perhaps it was the sound of the saw that drew Ben in, the way it hummed and screeched. Perhaps it was the movement. Perhaps he leaned closer to watch his uncle more carefully, to see better; after all, it was his chair. Perhaps it had to do with his age and his desire to touch, touch, touch, exploring anything that glinted or shone or spun or ticked, exploring everything that even fleetingly captured his attention.

Perhaps his uncle only looked up for a split second, or blinked too long, or turned away to sneeze. But that was all it took.

Although Ben didn't remember the day, he was told the story long ago—the facts of it—and maybe he made part of it up, too, so that what he knew about the accident he recalled as in a silver dream. But it was not discussed, and it was not something he thought about often or dwelled on. Of course, he received occasional stares from strangers, and for a brief time he was fondly known as Alien Boy to his best friends, but because he had grown up with nine fingers, the space on his hand was just a space, no more, no less, like the hole left after a tooth is pulled.

≈   ≈

Ben could not remember the last time Uncle Ian's name had been mentioned, or when he had even been indirectly referred to. With the arrival of the letter, it occurred to Ben that the silence about Uncle Ian was a real thing, the absence was a presence. His uncle was a cloistered part of their lives, but Ben sensed that changing forever as he watched his mother read the letter.

Her eyebrows rose and dropped like a twitch, then her face shifted and fell to blankness. She continued to read and when she had finished, she sighed, looking down and to the side.

Ben waited. He knew when not to say anything.

Because he was still out of breath from rushing to his parents' store, his chest heaved.

"We can't afford the time to go," she said finally. "You know, the store." Her tone was cautious. "And I don't want you to go alone."

"Why?" he asked quietly.

After a moment she shrugged. "I really don't want to talk about it right now. I'm just sorry this happened on your birthday."

"I'm not."

She seemed stung by this comment, and Ben tried to choose his words carefully, but he had a hard time holding back. "Mom, this is my only uncle, my long-lost fugitive uncle, my only relative except for you guys and Gramma Lu...." His voice cracked, excited, then trailed off as he saw her eyes rest on his left hand. Nonchalantly, he slid his left hand behind his right. "Don't even worry about the finger thing. If *I'm* not mad about it, you shouldn't be."

The bell on the front door rang, announcing someone coming or going.

"It's a free vacation," Ben joked, trying to make his mother laugh, something he was usually very good at.

"You can't understand," she said simply, oblivious to his attempt at lightheartedness. "And I don't expect you to."

The letter lay open between them on the ancient, wavy pine table at the far end of the store office. The paint on the table was robin's-egg blue and blistering.

When Ben was little, he often amused himself while his parents worked by pretending that the tabletop was a great sea, the deck of cards stored inside the table's one drawer was his personal fleet of fifty-two ships, and he was an admiral. Kneeling on a chair piled with oversize books, he guided the ships through dangerous waters infested with sleek paper-clip sharks and translucent cough-drop stingrays.

All at once, Ben's mother grabbed the letter. "Wait here," she said, holding the letter away from her body. "I'll be right back. I'll see if your father's done up front. I want him to read this."

"Okay."

She moved purposefully through the office, negotiating the maze of book cartons.

With his thumbnail, Ben broke open a cracking bubble of paint on the table. He blew the paint chips aside to reveal a honey-colored patch of wood. He wondered how much he didn't know about his uncle, how much his mother did. He decided that his mother was a bottle of secrets, and he wanted to know everything he deserved to know.

≈   ≈

About ten minutes later, Ben's father entered the office alone, tapping the folded letter against his thigh.

"Where's Mom?" Ben asked.

"With a customer," his father answered. "Someone looking for a cookbook who did not want to be waited on by a man. Weird," he added, shaking his head in disbelief.

Ben was still at the table, sitting now. He had been counting the money in his wallet again for something to do while he waited. Jerkily, he flipped the wallet shut and replaced it in his pocket. He gulped before he spoke. "Well, what do you think?"

His father slid the letter across the table to Ben. "Yours," he said. "What do I think—I think this is a pretty emotional thing for your mother. It was all so sudden. Give her some time."

"But what do *you* think?"

"It's not up to me. Ian's your mother's brother."

"Dad, you can still *think* something."

"Oh, I don't know." One corner of his father's mouth curved up toward a smile. "I suppose I'd like to see him again," he said with an aimless wave. "After all, he is family. And there aren't very many of us, that's for sure. But you and I don't know what it's like to have a brother or sister, so—" He broke off as though a new thought had come to him, making him forget what he was about to say.

"But it should be up to *me*," Ben said. "I mean, the envelope has *my* name on it."

His father drew in his shoulders. "Well, actually, that's part of the problem. Your mother thinks Ian should have written to *her*."

The air conditioner kicked in loudly, causing both their heads to turn. The roar filled the room, sounding to Ben as if they were under the hood of a speeding car. The initial blast quieted to a low murmur. Outside, drips from the old machine were forming a small pond that had begun to creep under the back door.

"Stupid thing," his father muttered, sneering at the air conditioner. "I wish one of us was a mechanical wizard and could fix that damn contraption." He puffed up his cheeks, exhaled noisily. "Really, though . . ." he said, looking directly at his son, then pausing. "It's more than the accident, you know. Your mother and Ian have never been close. They've had a lot of issues over the years. Long before you were born. The accident just tipped the scales."

Ben straightened a little in his chair. None of that mattered to him. "I think I want to go to Oregon," he told his father.

"I can see that."

"Will you help me? With Mom?"

Ben's father's eyes flashed and he moved his head. Almost a nod.

≈　≈

Why did he want to go so badly? He had never wanted it before. But he hadn't even finished reading the letter when that started to change. Things kept changing all day long. He looked at his hand differently. Was it ugly? He looked at his mother differently. Rarely did he think of her as someone's sister.

18

He tried to remember anything connected to the accident, but came up with little.

"Don't worry, Mama. It'll grow back." He knew those words, but he must have been told them as part of the story of the accident.

He remembered wanting to be a cartoonist after discovering with great joy that a good number of cartoon characters—Mickey Mouse included—had only four fingers on each hand. But his character, his own creation, would have nine fingers. Four on one hand, five on the other.

He remembered his parents taking him to a Diego Rivera show at a museum in Chicago. Or was it Milwaukee? In one of the rooms, mural studies were displayed. Pages and pages of charcoal drawings of hands. Solid, broad, perfect hands as big as suitcases. It had made him dizzy.

His thoughts kept returning to his uncle. Who wouldn't want to meet the person responsible? Wasn't it more weird not to think about it?

After all those years, Ben found himself curious. He couldn't ignore the feeling. It was like a tiny ache blooming behind his ears and spreading slowly throughout his head.

Maybe by morning it would be gone. But it wasn't. It layered his dreams and fell heavily across his mind the next day.

3

THE PAINTING was simple. The picture plane was divided in half. The top half was sky—creamy yellow, the color of butter. The bottom half was dark green, almost black, interrupted by an oval the same color as the sky: a small pond. Ben had painted a single leafless tree breaking the horizon. The branches were ragged and angular, tapering off into sharp points. Dissatisfied with the tree, Ben instinctively painted over it with dark green, feathering the edges out. It ended up a mound like a large haystack or a tiny hill, backlit, at dusk or dawn, a time of change.

Ben had known it was a success as soon as he had finished, and he was pleased, the way he was pleased after acing a test in math class or sinking nine out of ten free throws in gym.

"It's gorgeous," his mother had said, tipping her head and craning her neck to study the brushwork. She smiled.

"It's one of the nicest paintings I've ever seen," his father had ventured to say. He rested his hands on Ben's shoulders, his chin on Ben's head. "I like the way the shape of the hill echoes the shape of the pond. You're good. You are very good."

Ben had painted *Yellow Sky* at the kitchen table, last October, for extra credit for art class. His teacher, Ms. Temple, was so impressed by it, she entered it in a competition. Ben won first prize for the city, then the region, and finally for the entire state. In April, he had his photograph taken with the governor at the capitol, where he was awarded a blue satin ribbon, a certificate with his name written in fancy script, and a savings bond for fifty dollars. The photograph appeared in newspapers all over Wisconsin. Even Gramma Lu's newspaper carried it.

Afterward his parents framed *Yellow Sky* and hung it above the fireplace, replacing a weaving that Ben's mother had done in college. Many times a day Ben passed it, sometimes noticing it, sometimes not.

Ben's mother had even tried to arrange for private lessons for him with a painting professor at the university, a professor whose work she particularly admired. She made an appointment with the man and showed him a portfolio of Ben's work. Ben was relieved to hear that the professor had politely declined, stating that his busy schedule wouldn't allow it.

"But he said you were extremely talented." His mother had glowed as she reported that bit of information. "Gifted."

"Whatever," was Ben's weak response.

During the first days that followed Ben's birthday, the idea of a studio of his own became more and more of a burden to him. He didn't want the room. He didn't want to feel pressured into being an artist. Although Ben liked art, he had no real desire to "be" anything, much less an artist. What about a basketball player? Or a journalist? Or some kind of professional traveler, if there was such a thing? Occasionally he imagined taking over his parents' bookstore one day. But there were too many choices for him to be narrowed down so soon. And if it took as long as it had to reach age twelve, it would be forever until he needed to decide what he wanted to do with his life.

Ben wished he had never painted *Yellow Sky*.

≈   ≈

Another blank white day had become a still, hot night, continuing the endless pattern. The moon was nearly full with a blurred halo—a dandelion gone to seed. Ben and his mother were sitting out on the front steps. Ben's father was up in his new studio; jazz from his CD player drifted down to them, a comfort to Ben, the next best thing to having his father right there.

Ben ran a sweaty can of cream soda along his calf until he shivered. He wiggled around and settled himself on the concrete stoop. Already, Ben had gone back inside the house three times. Once to turn off the porch light that was drawing so many bugs it looked like a prop for a horror movie. Once to get another can of cream soda for himself and the bottle of red wine from the kitchen counter for his mother. And lastly to search for insect repellent to ward off the mosquitoes. They bothered Ben much more than his parents. Itchy red bites dotted his arms and legs.

"Do you think he's writing?" his mother asked, tilting her head upward.

"Maybe."

"I hope so. I think he's a fine writer. I'd love for him to have some luck with it. Some success."

"Yeah." Ben was trying to think of a way to change the subject. Talking about his father's writing could easily lead to talking about his father's new studio, which, in turn, could easily lead to talking about Ben's new room—a subject he wanted to avoid.

It was four days after Ben's birthday, and he had avoided it fairly well so far. His mother had been avoiding something, too; she had been avoiding the subject of Uncle Ian.

"Dad's music must be on pretty loud," Ben said. "I mean, if we can hear it with the windows shut and the air conditioner cranking."

"Well, at least he's actually *in* his studio. That's more than I can say. If I'm in mine for more than five minutes, I can't bear it and I have to leave." His mother clinked her teeth against the rim of her wineglass. "I look around my beautiful new studio—all set up and ready to go, the warp strung on my loom—but I can't seem to get moving. I tell myself I'm tired from working at the store, but I suppose it's more than that."

"Hmm." Ben didn't know how else to respond.

"But that's not why I asked you to stay home tonight," she said. "I know you'd rather be hanging out with Brian and Jamie, but we need to talk about Uncle Ian."

Ben had been anticipating this. "No big deal," he replied. "Brian and Jamie will live without me for one night." He could picture them meeting at the university, down in back of the student union building by the lake. That had been their plan. They were going to see what fun they could have with the plastic turds and rubber puddle of vomit Brian and Jamie had given Ben for his birthday. Ben had loaned his gifts to his friends for the evening, hoping they wouldn't lose them.

Ben's mother refilled her glass. "Okay," she began. "Here goes . . ." She took a sip of wine, then twirled the glass as she spoke. "Even when we were small— growing up—Uncle Ian and I were never very . . . oh . . . connected. I always thought brothers and sisters should share some special bond or something, but we didn't. We were forever at each other, arguing constantly about any old thing. I guess I'd have to say that I always loved him, but I really didn't like him very much."

"Can you be more specific?" Ben asked. These were the exact words his mother had said to him many times during discussions that had started too broadly, or in vagueness, discussions that needed her guidance if the two of them were ever to get to the point.

"Sure. I remember him pushing me off the swing in the backyard on a regular basis—that's how I broke my arm. I remember him getting so mad at me when your grandpa showed me even a teensy bit of favoritism that he would pull my hair or pinch my legs. I remember him drawing a mustache on my official Bobby Sherman fan-club photo. With permanent marker."

"Who?"

"Oh, no one you'd know or care about." She laughed. "Just shows how old I am."

"Ancient."

"Thank you," she said, the laugh lingering. She went on, serious again, "When we were in high school, he poured bleach on my favorite pair of blue jeans, ruining them. I cried over that one. I cried a lot, I guess." With her free hand she waved away a moth, thick as a chunk of bread. It flitted against the railing, then melted into the darkness. "He used to call me Judy instead of Julie, for years, just to spite me. I *hated* that. God, did I hate that. He never did it in front of Grandma or Grandpa, and I was never certain if they believed me or not when I complained about it."

None of this seemed out of the ordinary to Ben. Jamie and his brother Gil were always fighting—verbally and physically. Sometimes they pounded each other so hard they sported bruises on their arms for weeks. The bruises were purplish blue like grape juice stains or tattoos of delphiniums. "Sounds like normal stuff to me."

His mother shrugged. "Those may not seem like terrible things, but it's funny to me that I can't remember nice things. Just unpleasant ones. It always seemed to me that he was a wall keeping me from day-to-day happiness."

Silence.

Ben wagged the fingers on his left hand. There was enough light from the moon and the street lamp to cast a faint shadow. The shadow looked like an octopus with the wrong number of tentacles, moving frantically but getting nowhere. "So that's it?"

"What?" She was miles away.

"So you fought with your brother when you were kids. Big deal, Mom. I mean, that's no reason not to talk to him. And this," Ben said, tossing his hand out toward her, "was an accident."

"Ben? Stop." She steadied his hand.

"Tell me everything. You have to."

"Listen, there's so much, too much, to go into. And it doesn't concern you."

"But don't you see, Mom? It does. It's *my* birthday gift. And I'm *twelve* now."

"Yes, you are." Ben's mother brushed her bangs out of her eyes, then did the same to him. "Well, you know the background material, and the rest is just more of the same." She swallowed some wine and forged ahead in a voice that lifted and dropped depending on what she was saying. Some things Ben had heard before (the things about his grandparents), but most he had not.

She told Ben again about the car crash that had killed his grandmother when his mother was twenty-one years old and Ian was nineteen. And how she had volunteered to drop out of college to work at her father's bookstore and to live at home, cooking his favorite meals and playing the piano for him at night, helping him through his grief. She didn't see Ian for weeks on end even though his dormitory was only a mile or so away, and she wanted him to be with them if for nothing else but to take up space in the dreary house.

She told Ben that later when her father was diagnosed with cancer and grew sicker, Ian drifted farther and farther away, taking off when she needed him most, borrowing money from their father, quitting college for the last time, and traveling all over the country and Europe, only showing up at the very end when it was too late.

She said: "Someone had to be responsible."

She said: "If it wasn't for your father, I don't know what I would have done."

She said: "And you, having you got me through."

Ben knew that his grandfather had died two days after he was born, as though his grandfather had been hanging on to welcome his only grandchild.

By this time, his mother had set the wineglass down and had folded her arms. "Your birth and his death were all tangled together for me," she said, blinking her eyes several times. "And that's when Ian decided to stay in Madison. Grandpa had given the store to Dad and me, and—"

"Maybe Uncle Ian wanted the store, too?"

"No. No, he didn't. He just wanted money. He had been learning how to make furniture on his travels. And he used his inheritance to put a down payment on a tiny house and to buy woodworking equipment." She paused. "I think we tried to be a family for a while. I baked bread for him, and he offered to baby-sit from time to time. But it was always strained. We never talked about anything that mattered."

"How many times do you think I saw him? How many times did he baby-sit me?"

"Oh, I really couldn't say. Seven or eight times, I guess."

"I don't remember him."

"You were too little."

"And then?"

"And then the accident happened. After that it was just too difficult for the two of us to be together. We saw less and less of each other. And then he moved.

First to California, where we stayed in touch for a while, and then I heard from an old family friend that he was in Oregon, but I never knew for certain."

"Now we do."

She nodded, then gazed off into the distance without focus. "But it doesn't change things."

Ben glanced at his mother. In the shadows and with her head angled away, the curve of her cheek was puffy like a berry. He couldn't see her expression. But he could guess what it was. Ben knew that his mother was done dredging up memories, and it was clear that what she had told him was to her mind a solid explanation for choosing not to go to Oregon.

"There," she sighed, turning back, her eyes sharp. "Enough said." She shot her chin forward, as if to strengthen her point. "Well, you've had an unusual birthday. At least you have one magnificent present, if I do say so myself."

"So what will you tell him when he calls?"

"*If* he calls—and I have a feeling it's a very big if— I'll just say thank you, and we can't do it right now."

"Oh." Ben turned her words over in his mind. He looked up at the moon. It was merely a ball caught in the tree branches, a spangle. Distance changed things, Ben thought. Distorted them. Of course, the moon was huge, but he would never really know that from this particular spot on the earth. And if his father hadn't taught him years ago that the moon shone by reflecting the sun's light, he might still assume that, from where he sat, the moon was conspicuous and electric of its own volition. How far is it from Wisconsin to Oregon? he wondered. Ben bit the inside of his cheek. He squirmed; every inch of him felt fidgety. He had something he needed to clear up. "Mom?" he said cautiously.

"Hmm?"

"Mom, if I had to choose, I'd take the trip over the room." Somehow, saying it like that seemed less harsh than saying "I don't want the room." But it was still the truth, and his parents had always taught him that it was never a mistake to tell the truth. It was always the reasonable thing to do.

"Really?" Her voice had risen and her head jerked a little.

Ben nodded. He tugged on his collar, scratched his legs.

"You're not kidding, are you?"

"No," Ben whispered.

"Huh. Well . . ." Her eyes darted away from him toward a house across the street, its windows lit up, amber. He could see her jaw tighten.

"I'm sorry, Mom," Ben told her in the thinnest of voices. He was on the verge of tears: a curse of being his age.

"Don't be sorry. It's not something to be sorry about. I'm just glad you told me."

The air was motionless, as though his house, his

street, his neighborhood had been tucked inside a box and tightly sealed.

Ben's mother smoothed her hands absently over her arms. Then, with a gentle shove, she directed him toward the front door. "Go, go," she told him. "I'll be in in a few minutes."

The cool blast of indoor air met Ben like a wall. He stood on the threshold, separating the cold and the light within the house from the heat and the darkness without. Soon he would drift off to his room and to sleep, a bit relieved for having been honest, and a bit something else, but what he didn't know. Sad for his mother? But first he pressed his forehead to the screen, watching her. Bleached by the moonlight, she wandered onto the lawn and froze for a moment like a statue in a formal garden. Then, taking slow, swaying steps, she disappeared behind the black shape of the hedge.

≈   ≈

It was decided three days later: Ben and his mother would make the trip to Oregon, and Ben's father would stay home to take care of the bookstore. The knowledge that they were actually going ticked inside Ben like a clock.

"I can't promise you anything more than a disaster," his mother had said with a half smile, as a footnote to her announcement.

"I love a good disaster," Ben replied, a comment that

downplayed his disbelief. He gave his mother a tremendous hug. "Thank you."

His mother drew a long breath and exhaled upward, her lower lip protruding, her bangs fanning out. "Just bear with me," she told him. "I mean it." Then she laughed—a soft, kind laugh.

Two weeks after that, at dusk, Ben and his mother were thirty-five thousand feet above the ground, over a smattering of clouds, somewhere between Wisconsin and Oregon. They were flying, heading west toward the sinking sun, which burst at the horizon like a magnificent poppy.

Ben was so entranced by the color spreading across the sky that he forgot he was having a conversation with his mother. He only heard the end of what she was saying.

". . . and it's a feeling I can summon up immediately," she finished, and then she, too, saw the sky over his shoulder and out the window, and couldn't help but smile.

Part Two

THERE

4

SAME WALK, same hands, same worried forehead. Same droop of the shoulders, same tilt of the head.

Ben recognized his uncle instantly, because looking at the man approaching them in the airport terminal was like looking at his mother through the dense, swirly glass of the French doors between the living room and dining room.

Same long nose, same pale gray eyes, same thin coppery hair.

The three of them took in one another without blinking, saying nothing. After a long moment, Ben said shyly, "Uncle Ian," and stepped forward. His mother shadowed him, joining him in a tentative hug with Ian. The uncle. The brother.

Three voices all at once: "Hi." "Hi." "Hi."

And then Ian said firmly, "I am so happy to see you. Both," he added in a whisper. His eyes seemed to be following an invisible bird from Ben's mother's shoes to Ben's shoulder to an exit sign above their heads and away. He rubbed his chin, then ran his thumb along his eyebrow.

Ben's mother nodded with pursed lips.

"Me, too," said Ben. Suddenly he became aware of his hand and jammed it into his pocket. But that seemed awkward. He pulled it out, letting it drop at his side like a weight.

"It's too bad that Ed couldn't come with you," said Ian.

"Yes," said Ben's mother. "He wanted to. The store, you know. Someone had to be there."

Ian coughed. "I know."

"He sends his love."

They hadn't moved. The waiting area was emptying. People rushed by, alone and in clusters, colored blurs vanishing down the long hallway. At the fringe of his vision, Ben spotted a joyful reunion with tears and hugs and balloons and flowers and flashing cameras and a banner that read WELCOME HOME, BUNNY! Ben hadn't quite pictured that grand a production for his mother and uncle, but he had expected something more than what was happening right now.

"My throat's dry," said Ben's mother. "I could use some water. I'll be right back." She left them, walking briskly toward a drinking fountain several yards behind them.

Ben and Ian waited.

Ian shook his head. "You're all grown up."

"You are, too," Ben replied automatically. He couldn't believe how stupid he sounded. He blushed, his eyes circling shyly as if a proper response were hanging in the air. "I mean, you're a real person." The tips of his ears were bright red. Just as stupid, he thought.

"Yes, I am," said Ian, laughing.

The laughter broke the ice, released tension, and Ben laughed as well.

"What's so funny?" asked Ben's mother as she rejoined them. The corner of her mouth was wet and glistened when she stepped into the light. Her shoulder bag brushed against Ben's arm.

"Oh, nothing," said Ian.

"Nothing," echoed Ben.

"Let's get your luggage and head out," said Ian. "You two must be exhausted."

≈   ≈

The scent of pine laced the air, and the air was clear and cool and very different from the air in Wisconsin. Ben took deep breaths until he was light headed. He shivered.

He shivered again in the car, then sat absolutely still. His mother had nudged him into the front seat, saying, "You'll be able to see better. I'll sit in the back."

It's night, Ben thought, there isn't much to see.

The dark world out the windshield was open and big. Miles and miles away, a light was moving across the sky. The space inside the car was made smaller by the uncertainty of how things would turn out and by what seemed like shyness to Ben. Shyness all around.

But how could a brother and a sister be shy with each other? That made no sense to Ben.

"I—I'm married," Ian said. "I . . . wanted to tell you that before we got home." He spoke quietly, not stuttering exactly, but with hesitation. "You'll meet Nina. She's nice."

A ribbon of excitement shot through Ben. I have an aunt, he thought.

"You're *married*? I can't believe it." Ben's mother leaned forward, clutching the upholstery, one hand behind Ian's head, the other behind Ben's.

"It's true," said Ian. "We've been married for about a year, but we've been together for a long time." He had to smile.

"Congratulations, Ian."

"Yeah," said Ben. "That's cool." His mind stirred. The thought of the possibility of a cousin occurred to him.

"I checked for a wedding ring the minute I spotted you in the airport," said Ben's mother.

"I put it in my pocket," Ian explained. "I wanted to tell you before you said something to me."

Ben was twisting in his seat, watching them. The car's shoulder strap pulled against his neck as he moved. At first, Ben thought his mother was relaxing; she even seemed excited by Ian's news, but silence settled back over them quickly.

Ben pretended to sleep—head against the cold window, eyes darting about behind closed lids—with the intent of giving his mother and uncle some kind of privacy. But they only discussed the weather and the bookstore. After another silence, Ian shared impersonal facts about Nina at Ben's mother's request, both of them speaking in the low, even voices of polite strangers.

So tell me about her.

What?

Nina. How old is she?

A couple of years younger than me.

Where is she from?

California originally. That's where we met. We've been in Oregon for a few years now.

What does she do?

We work together. She paints the furniture I make.

From time to time Ben opened his eyes to mere slits, only to catch a glimpse of a passing car, seen and gone like a pulse. As the drive wore on, Ben peeked more often and for longer periods of time until he could pretend no longer. He feigned a yawn, then stared out at the Oregon night.

Soon Ian turned off the highway onto a narrow dirt road, hemmed in by a dark wall of trees. The trees thinned, and the road wound past a few outbuildings. Ian's voice found a different pitch. "Here we are," he announced. "We're home." The car came to a stop near a rustic cedar-shingled house.

Ben lumbered out of the car, stretched, and looked around.

Lights were on inside the house, and there were many uncovered windows. The house appeared before them like a lantern, glowing brightly in the middle of a thicket at the end of the world.

"I'll give you a tour of the place tomorrow," Ian told them, motioning with his head and arm toward the sweep of hills and trees that surrounded them and folded into the night.

They gathered their bags and walked up a stone path to the front door.

Just prior to entering the house, Ben asked his uncle one question: "Do I have a cousin?"

"Not yet," was the answer.

≈   ≈

Ben watched his mother and aunt embrace. He had a hard time directing his eyes away from Nina's belly, despite the fact that looking at her embarrassed him enormously. When she hugged him, he held his breath. It was an awkward hug due to her size.

Nina was wearing a pale orange jumper and all Ben could think was: giant cantaloupe.

"It's a pleasure to meet you, Benjamin," she said.

"Me, too. You can call me Ben," he added.

"Ben," she said, nodding. Her skin was pink and smooth, and something about her conveyed the words *welcoming* and *kind.*

Nina had yawned about a dozen times since Ian had

introduced her, just minutes earlier. She yawned again. "Excuse me. Exhaustion seems to be a big part of this pregnancy. I'm usually in bed by now, but I wanted to wait up for your arrival. But if I don't go to bed soon, I'm going to fall asleep right here, standing up, like a horse. Good night..."

Ben blinked. And she was gone. Blink. Some of the lights had been turned off. Blink. What time was it? How late?

Before it had fully registered with Ben, he was alone downstairs. The greetings were done. The sleeping arrangements were figured out. Ben and his mother had called home to say they had arrived safely. Ian had gone upstairs to join Nina. And Ben's mother had retired to the small upstairs room that would eventually become the new baby's nursery.

Ben had been given a choice—he could either sleep on the sofa or on a cot out on the screened back porch. It was chilly, but the idea of being on the porch appealed to him. He wandered through the rooms, acquainting himself with the house, before he settled in for the night.

The travel and the anticipation had worn him out. He blinked to stay awake. And he blinked as though his eyelids were shutters, his mind a camera, and he was capturing this new place and storing it away. The kitchen with its knotted, wide-planked floor that pitched down toward the sink. The living room with its stone fireplace—round and gaping like the mouth of a lion. And the dining room—each of the four walls had been painted a different color, and one wall, the largest, unbroken one, was covered entirely with photographs. Except for Ian and Nina, Ben didn't recognize anyone in the photographs, but he was too tired to spend much time looking.

Ben guessed that most of the furniture in the house had been made by Ian. He examined one chest of drawers closely. The chest had twelve square drawers, four rows of three. Each drawer had a grooved surface; the grooves were painted in alternating, muted colors— green, blue, gray; green, blue, gray. It reminded Ben of a patchwork quilt. It amazed him to think that his uncle had built it.

The floor creaked as Ben walked quietly to the porch.

As he made himself comfortable under some blankets and a down comforter, he was thinking of his father, home alone. But it was one of the photographs he was picturing as he crossed over to sleep. In the photograph, five children of descending height, dressed in old-fashioned clothes, bent slightly forward, backs to the viewer, were looking through curtained French doors, captivated by the intense white light that shone through. Ben knew they were brothers and sisters. He wondered what that felt like.

5

"THERE HE IS," said a voice.

"There he is," a slightly higher but similar voice repeated.

The first voice: "I see him."

The second: "I see him."

Ben awoke and lifted his head to the sunlight, cocked his head toward the sound of giggling. His eyes focused in time to see two white-haired children running away from the porch and out of sight. Peals of silly laughter trailed behind them through the piney brush.

Ben sat up and rubbed his eyes with the heel of his hand. Had he been dreaming? One, two, three——he sprang from bed, pulled on his jeans and hiking boots, and passed from room to room of the house through bands of light and shadow. He was drawn to the kitchen by the smells of coffee and fresh bakery, and by the soft rumble of conversation.

Ian was standing by the sink, and Ben's mother was across the room, leaning against the counter beside a plate of muffins. Both held mugs of coffee.

"Morning," Ben called. He was surprised to see his

mother up and dressed before he was, when she didn't have to be.

"Hey, here's the artist," said Ian cheerfully.

Ben stopped and slipped his mother an angry look. "Mom?"

"What?" said his mother. "I was just telling Ian about your art prizes. He's an artist—I thought it would interest him."

Ben rolled his eyes.

"It does," said Ian. "Congratulations. That's terrific. At your age, I was doing nothing but wasting time. I'd love to see your paintings someday. Your mother says you're very good."

"I'm okay—at art—I guess," he told Ian. Then he faced his mother. "Mom, didn't you know it's impolite to talk about someone behind his back?"

Ian squared his shoulders. "Don't blame your mother. I was asking questions about you. And . . . well, it's easier to talk about you than it is to talk about us—your mother and me." His right eyebrow arched as he said it.

His mother averted her eyes and ran her finger around the rim of her mug. She shrugged. "True," she whispered.

For a second, Ben felt uncomfortable, as though he were an adult and the adults were children. "Where's Aunt Nina?" he thought to ask.

"She's off on her morning walk," said Ian.

"And she's already baked these muffins," said Ben's mother. "They're delicious. I know—I've had two."

"Why don't *we* go for a walk?" suggested Ian. "Grab a muffin, Ben, and let me get a coffee refill. Maybe we'll bump into Nina. If nothing else, you'll get to see the place. Julie, you, too? You can work off your breakfast."

Ben saw them scowl at each other, and he couldn't tell if the scowls were meant to be playful or not.

They walked and walked, taking a twisty course toward the border of Ian and Nina's land. At the property line, they began a circle, following a well-worn path that ran along the fringe of the woods, and, for a good stretch, edged sweet-smelling orchards—peach and apple. The distant hills were tawny with a nap, and perfectly shaped, like upside-down bowls. The circle halfway completed, the three of them cut back to the house and the cluster of outbuildings by threading through growths of scruffy trees.

Ian's short, descriptive comments about the trees and the land were spaced by lengthy pauses. During the pauses, Ben meant to ask about the children he had glimpsed as he awoke, but remained silent, eating two of Nina's muffins and watching his mother and uncle.

Throughout the walk, Ben continually found himself between them. Even if he slowed down and parted some branches to look at something that had caught his eye, or jogged ahead to peer around a bend to check for Nina, they would slow down or speed up, too, and shuffle about to let him back in place, separating them.

Ian pointed out the long shed in which Nina painted the furniture. "It used to be a broken-down chicken coop," he explained. "I fixed it up." One would never sense the shed's former incarnation. It looked immaculate now, brand-new. "And that's where I store some of my wood," he told them, indicating a sturdy box of a building, covered in vines.

Gesturing toward the remaining building in the grouping, Ben's mother said, "Then that must be your studio." The building was very much like the house. It was nearly the same size as the house, and had the same cedar-shingled exterior, same silver-gray roof, and numerous windows. But, unlike the house's windows, these were so tall they reached up two stories, mirroring an expanse of sky. "Do we get to see it?"

"Do you want to see it?" Ian said softly.

"I wouldn't have asked if I didn't," she replied.

Ben nodded.

Ian led them to the studio via a trampled footway. He flung the remains of his coffee into a wave of wildflowers and set his mug down in a patch of high grass near the wide front door. He unlocked the door and opened it without a sound. They stepped into a sunny room that was as clean and carefully organized as a museum.

"You never used to be so neat," said Ben's mother.

Ian shrugged. "Live and learn."

A massive, thick, wooden workbench was an island in the room around which everything else orbited. Hand tools—chisels, mallets, gouges, hammers, clamps, planes, and saws—hung from the walls. Screws and other hardware were stored like specimens, in glass jars, in rows on narrow shelves. Ben saw sanders, different kinds of drills, and some power tools and machines he couldn't name. The table saw was covered with a black plastic tarp. There didn't seem to be sawdust or wool shavings anywhere, no works in progress, but the good smell of wood was present. The stillness, the shrouded table saw, the openness of the space, and the shafts of sunlight dramatically streaming down made Ben feel as though he were standing in the nave of a church.

"Great room," said Ben, expecting to hear an echo.

Ian nodded. "Thank you. I like it."

Ben's mother passed her hand along the edge of the workbench. "Our new attic rooms I was telling you about are minuscule in comparison to this," she said.

"This is the first big studio I've had," Ian said, gazing out one of the large windows.

Ben wondered what had happened to the chair Ian

had been finishing when the accident occurred. It struck Ben that he wouldn't recognize the chair if he saw it; he knew nothing about it, except that it must be small, made for a two-year-old. "What are you working on?"

"Nothing right now," Ian answered. "I've got a show in New York next month, and all my new pieces have already been shipped to the gallery. I always take a break after I send off the new work for a show. And I couldn't have planned things better if I tried—I had intended to take a long break around the time of the baby's due date, anyway." Ian laced his fingers together. "Would you like to see a catalog for the show? They just arrived."

"Sure," said Ben.

Ian walked to a file cabinet in the corner of the studio and pulled two catalogs off the top of a tall stack. He handed one each to Ben and his mother.

Ben's mother flipped through hers quickly and returned it to the stack.

Ben paged through his slowly, reading the titles of the pieces, studying the photographs of the chests and cabinets, trying to picture them in three dimensions.

"You may keep that," said Ian, fiddling about with his keys. He moved closer and closer to the door, as if he were trying, in a subtle way, to get them to leave.

"Thanks," said Ben. He snapped the catalog shut, and at the same moment the door swung open.

The two children Ben had seen earlier blew into the room, all elbows and knees. Knobby little things. Directly behind them was a girl approximately Ben's age, out of breath and apologetic.

"I'm sorry, Ian," said the girl, puffing. "They got away from me. Again." She snatched the children's hands. "You guys know the studio's off-limits. Come on," she demanded, pulling them outside.

In the open air, they all gathered together along with Nina, who had just arrived, forming a loose, lopsided ring, half in sun, half in shade.

"I found the twins on my walk," said Nina. "And they really wanted to meet Ben. And they are *fast*."

The twins became shy all of a sudden. They scrambled in back of Nina. First their fists, and then their towheads, peeked out from behind Nina's tentlike dress, which was patterned with pale blue forget-me-nots.

"We're the Deeters," said the older girl. "I'm Lynnie, and these are the twi—"

"I'm Kale!" the boy piped.

"I'm Elka!" chirped the girl.

"We're five years old—a whole hand," Kale told Ben, thrusting his hand at him, the grimy fingers splayed. "Lynnie's thirteen."

Ian tapped Ben's shoulder, lightly and briefly. "This is my nephew, Ben, and his mother, my sister, Julie. They live in Wisconsin."

"We knew you were coming," said Kale.

"We did," said Elka. "Ian told us."

"We saw you on the porch."

"We did. You were sleeping."

Lynnie rolled her eyes and hiked up her shoulders, as if to say: I know they're annoying. Forgive me.

Her name repeated in Ben's mind, ruining his concentration. *Lynnie Deeter. Lynnie Deeter* . . .

"Kale, Elka, and Lynnie live over in the apple orchard," Ian told Ben and his mother. "Very near where we just walked. Their parents, grandparents, and uncle own the apple orchard. The peach and pear orchards, as well."

"They're *mine*, too," said Kale, poking himself in the chest.

"Living in an orchard sounds romantic," said Ben's mother. "Like something out of a novel."

"It's mostly hard and dirty work," Lynnie said shyly. "You should smell my dad at the end of the day."

Giggles.

After a few questions for Ben, asked urgently with wide, curious eyes—"How old are you? Are you moving here? Do you like apples?"—Kale and Elka got squirmy. They pulled at Lynnie.

"Come on," insisted Kale. "We have to work on the baby present."

"It's *really* big," Elka volunteered, spreading her

bony arms as far apart as she could. "Way too big to wrap."

"Shhh," hissed Kale. He was so close to Elka, his nose grazed her cheek. "Lynnie, we don't have much time left." He pushed out his lower lip, waiting.

"You have about four weeks," said Nina, looking downward, a sweet expression on her face. "Don't worry; take your time." A staccato breeze rippled her dress, and, for the first time, Ben thought of the actual baby inside her, swimming and floating.

Kale and Elka were shifting from foot to foot and hopping in place and generally acting like popcorn popping.

Lynnie let out a sigh. "Well, I guess I'd better go," she said. "I'm getting paid to watch them." She wrinkled her mouth and nose at her siblings.

"Lynnie," said Ian, "ask your parents if the three of you can come by for dinner tonight. That way Ben won't have to spend the entire evening with stuffy adults."

Nina jabbed at him. "Stuffy? Speak for yourself."

"Yes," Ben's mother agreed.

"Great. I'll ask," said Lynnie. "What time?"

"Oh, how about six?"

"Okay," Lynnie replied over her shoulder, already on her way. "And thank you."

"Bye," Ben called, watching them run down the

hilly path. The twins were on either side of Lynnie, their fingers hooked through her belt loops; like determined little tugboats, they steered her over the gentle risings.

Ben's mother, Nina, and Ian headed back toward the house. Ben lagged behind, fanning himself with Ian's catalog. He noticed that Nina was now the person in between, just as he had been. As he ran to catch up with them, he heard his mother laugh—a real laugh, a throaty one, void of nervousness or hesitancy, the first real laugh he'd heard from her since the arrival of Ian's letter. He took it as a good sign.

6

THEY HAD A PLEASANT, low-keyed lunch, during which Ben learned things.

He learned that although Nina had spent most of her childhood in northern California, her family had lived on a houseboat on Puget Sound the year she was ten. He learned that she had an older sister, a brother-in-law, and two nephews, and that they all—her parents included—lived in San Diego now.

He learned that Ian was still a Milwaukee Brewers fan, even though the Seattle Mariners, his home team, were playing much better than the Brewers. Ian vaguely recalled when the Braves were still in Milwaukee, and brought out a toddler-size T-shirt printed with the logo to prove it. He placed the faded shirt on the table between the dishes, never letting go of the unraveling bottom hem. "God, I remember that shirt," Ben's mother whispered, idly touching the sleeve, forming a connection.

He learned that Ian and Nina had gotten married in Ian's studio on a wet October afternoon with only a handful of friends and a judge present. Ian said, "With the big windows showing a watery sky, it felt as if we were under the sea." Nina said, "We had to wait for a lull in the rain to say our vows, because the drumming on the roof was so loud no one could hear us."

Ben wasn't particularly interested in wedding details, but he listened intently to everything said and joined in when it felt right. By degrees, he was getting to know this new part of his family.

≈ ≈

After lunch, Ben found a sketchbook propped against his backpack on the screened porch. The sketchbook was bound in dimpled black leather, and had a red ribbon bookmark attached at the spine. He opened it and riffled through it to see if there were any clues as to who had placed it there. No card or note had been tucked into the thickness of pages; there was no inscription.

With the sketchbook under his arm, he marched into the kitchen. But before he could hold it up and ask, "Does anyone know anything about this?" Ian said, "Oh, that's from me. An artist should never be without a sketchbook. I slipped it onto the porch by your things while you and Nina were clearing the dishes."

"Thanks," Ben said readily. It was much easier to accept a sketchbook than it was to accept a room.

"Sometimes I go through one of those in a week."

"You do? But you make furniture."

"Well, I work out all my design ideas on paper before I start with wood. But I'm constantly sketching—anything and everything. Mostly I'm inspired by forms in nature—trees, rocks, leaves. And by the textures of those things—bark, for example. I have two sketchbooks completely filled with drawings of bark. I did a series of chests a few years ago in which the surfaces were carved to look like bark. All my sketching came in handy. Sketching keeps me—oh, aware."

"Hmm." Ben transferred the sketchbook from hand to hand. Sweat darkened the leather.

"Am I preaching? Sorry."

"No."

"Yes, you are," said Nina in a cheerful singsong. She and Ben's mother were hunched over the sink, separating a basketful of flowers into several unruly bouquets and wrestling the bouquets into vases. Ben noticed a white petal caught in his aunt's hair. "Ben, your uncle once gave me a sketchbook and a speech to go with it, but I—"

"Disappointed him sorely," Ian cut in, "by using it for telephone messages and grocery lists, ripping out the pages one by one."

Ian and Nina shared a knowing glance, and laughed.

"Speaking of grocery lists," said Nina. "Someone needs to go to town—to the store—before dinner. The list we made earlier is on the fridge."

"I'll go," said Ian.

"I'll go with you," Ben's mother said instantly.

Nina moved her hands in concentric circles around her belly. "Good," she said. "Then I'll take my nap."

Ian looked at his nephew. "Ben?"

Ben was thinking, deciding.

"You can stay here, if you want," his mother told him. "Right? Ian? Nina?"

"Sure," said Nina.

"Of course," said Ian.

"Do whatever you want, Ben," said his mother. "You're on vacation."

Because she had said yes to going so quickly, it seemed to Ben that his mother wanted to drive to town with Ian alone. "I'll stay here," he finally said. "Maybe I'll sketch."

He did. Or at least he tried to. After his mother and uncle drove away, he grabbed the sketchbook and a pencil and went outside. He walked straight to the orchards. He roamed the orchards; his eyes roamed, too. Looking. For something to draw? For the Deeters?

Several times he began a drawing—a cluster of ripening peaches, a gnarled apple tree, an explosion of clouds—but his heart wasn't in it, and so he gave up.

He wandered on. He avoided a small group of apple pickers. The pickers worked silently and diligently, using ladders that tapered and sacks that hung from their shoulders and sagged in front, big as his pregnant aunt.

At one point, he heard talking and laughter, and followed the sounds. As he closed in on the noises, he caught glimpses of the Deeters through the leaves— flashes of Kale and Elka's bright T-shirts, flickers of Lynnie's white one.

Something held him exactly where he was. Kept him from approaching, kept him from leaving. He stood still for quite a while.

I'll see them later, he thought. Soon. And he walked back to the house to wait for his family.

≈ ≈

Ben, who had been watching from the window, saw the Deeters coming, and opened the door for them. Kale and Elka sprang into the house in crazy leaps, their arms flapping, their voices piercing the air: "Boing, boing, boing!" Lynnie, carrying a plastic bucket of peaches, twisted past Ben, and as she did, their elbows knocked.

Lynnie's nearly invisible blond eyebrows jumped and settled. "Oops," she said.

"Sorry," said Ben, rubbing the spot, not because it smarted but because his hand was drawn to it instinctively. He could feel himself redden.

Lynnie smiled, her lips latched tightly. "For you," she said, offering the peaches. "For all of you guys."

"Thank you," Nina said from behind them, while Ben was still trying to get the words out.

"Yeah," Ben murmured. He took the peaches and gave them to Nina.

"They're beautiful," Nina commented as she led the way to the kitchen. "We'll have them for dessert, with ice cream." She raised the bucket, lowered her head, and inhaled. "Mmm." In the kitchen, she hunted for a place on the table to put the bucket, finally making room by shoving aside a pile of dinner plates and a brown paper bag filled with corn husks. "Lynnie, what kind are they? I like the different names of all the fruits."

Ben knew that there were different kinds of apples, but he just assumed that a peach was a peach.

"These are called Harmony," said Lynnie, with a certain pride. "The first of the Suncrests should be ready next week."

"Harmony," Nina repeated. "I like that. It sounds portentous."

Ben didn't know what portentous meant, but judging by the way he felt and the way all the food looked and smelled and the smile dividing Nina's face, it had to be something good.

≈   ≈

The food was delicious, and there was so much of it. Grilled salmon, sweet corn, pasta, salad, corn muffins, iced tea, and, for dessert, cookies, and, of course, peaches and ice cream. They ate outside. In the west, banks of clouds extended upward from the horizon like batting from a ripped seam. In the east, the clouds were puffy and constantly changing.

Ben ate more than he should have, but he had a hard time stopping, he was so caught up in the atmosphere. Somehow, the combination of people, food, and weather—the chemistry among them—had turned the picnic table and the surrounding yard into a big, sunny room of arrested time, into something as huge as the sky. He was so relaxed, he even told a joke, leaning into the table and using his hands for emphasis. Everyone laughed, but still, he sensed the eagerness in his own voice, and rather than tell another, he folded back into himself. He relaxed again. He ate a third ear of corn.

Kale and Elka made Ben chuckle with the goofy expressions on their faces and their silly pronouncements: "All peaches are men because they have fuzz, and fuzz is whiskers." "We're the fraterminal kind of twins. We came from two eggs. A boy one and a girl one." At one point, Elka peered gravely at Ben and whispered, "Icky Pee is gone." It was pure nonsense to Ben, but he paid her his undivided attention, maybe because he had never had a brother or sister. "Oh, yes," he replied in a very serious voice.

Blue veins could be seen beneath Kale's and Elka's pale skin like ballpoint pen tracings or blueprints showing through. They were so skinny and energetic, it was as though some mad, merry scientist had created them, cobbled them together—part sprite, part wood elf, part bird.

When Ben looked at Lynnie, he flexed his toes inside his shoes. There was a gap between her two front teeth; there was a patch of sunburn on her nose. She had changed clothes since he'd seen her earlier. Now she was wearing cutoff blue jeans over tights with pink and silver seashells on them. Her terry-cloth shirt was short; her belly button was visible. It was an outie. Ben had never seen one before.

While they waited for dessert, Lynnie studied the ends of her hair and braided some of the silky threads from the corn tassels. "What are you doing tomorrow?" she asked.

"I dunno," Ben answered. He sat forward, balancing on the very edge of the bench.

"I'll split my baby-sitting money with you if you help me watch the twins."

"Maybe. That'd be fun."

"Well, it never is fun exactly, but it would be better if you did it with me, that's for sure. After I've been with them for a while, I just click my brain off." She nibbled at her lip. "If I didn't, I'd spaz out."

"I'll think about it. I don't know if my mom or uncle have made any plans."

"Okay."

Dessert arrived in blue tin bowls and soon the bowls

were empty, and the time had come for the Deeters to go home. It seemed to Ben that no one wanted the evening to end. Good-byes were dragged out. Stalling, Elka asked to feel the baby kick, and then everyone took a turn. Ben was last.

"Do you want to give it a try?" Nina asked. "You don't have to if you don't want to."

"It's amazing," said Lynnie.

"I'd forgotten that sensation entirely," said Ben's mother.

Ben truly wanted to, although the thought of actually touching his new and only aunt's belly was enough to paralyze him. He stared at his right hand, the complete one. He willed his hand to move. Ever so slowly, it did. He watched his hand land on Nina's belly. His hand quivered. He could see the little movements ruffling Nina's dress, but to feel them sent a chill down his spine. Something about it made him uneasy. He remembered a scene from a movie in which an alien, inhabiting a human's body, burst forth through the person's stomach after a series of spasms and lurches. He withdrew his hand abruptly. "Wow," he said.

"It feels like a girl," said Elka.

Kale disagreed. "Boy."

"Some days I swear I have my own private ocean inside me," Nina said to the twins.

Elka pulled her knees together and lifted her heels off the ground—once, twice. She wove her fingers together and spoke to no one in particular. "My mama says that the baby can already see lights and hear things, so I almost told the baby what her big present from me and Kale is. But I didn't."

"Thank goodness," said Nina. "Keep it a surprise."

Ian was to walk the Deeters home, and Ben, his mother, and Nina would stay behind.

"Maybe I'll see you tomorrow," said Lynnie.

"Maybe," said Ben.

"Wait," Ben's mother called, approaching Ian. A paper napkin was stuck to the back of his shirt. She plucked it off. "I guess you still need me, little brother," she said, dangling the napkin for him to see.

Ian smiled. "I guess."

She waved good-bye, the napkin flapping from her fingertips.

Nina started collecting the dirty silverware in the empty salad bowl. She stifled a yawn, covering her mouth with a fist full of spoons.

"Nina," said Ben's mother, "why don't you put your feet up or go to bed? You did most of the cooking. We'll clean up."

"Are you sure?"

"Absolutely."

"Thank you," said Nina. "I won't argue with you." It was almost comical to Ben the way she waddled off to the house with as many things from the table as she could carry in one trip. "Good night."

"Night," Ben and his mother said at the same time.

There was a semicircle of Adirondack chairs near the picnic table. Ben's mother eased back into one. "Let's sit for a minute before we get to work," she said, flicking her sandals off.

"Today was a good day," said Ben. He plopped down into a chair, leaving one chair between them, empty.

"Mmm." Her eyes were closed, and her legs were stretched out. She tucked her hands under her elbows. "Are you having a good time?"

"Yeah," he answered, meaning it. "Are you?"

She opened her eyes. "I'm beginning to," she said, speaking slowly, as if she were choosing each word with extreme precision. "I think Ian really wanted— needed—to see me before they have the baby. He hasn't actually come right out and said that, but I strongly sense it, and that makes me happy." Her mouth widened slightly. A smile.

Ben nodded.

The bottommost clouds were brushed with yellow and pink. A band of pure light, like a molten river, ran along the tree line, demanding notice. They sat, perfectly contented, without sharing another word, while twilight lengthened. Stars were appearing when Ian came into view with the bouncing beam of a flashlight preceding him.

"Starlight, moonlight," sang Ian, "hope to see a ghost tonight..." He shone the flashlight on Ben's mother. "Remember that game we used to play with the neighborhood kids at dusk?"

"I'm not the ghost," she replied, not unpleasantly, squinting her eyes. "You're the one who vanished."

"Whatever," Ian said, snapping off the light.

Ben could feel his personal gauge of the day take a dip toward the uncomfortable zone. "What are we going to do tomorrow?" he asked quickly.

"Good question," said Ian. He eyed the empty chair between them, but remained standing. "I was thinking—since you're not here for very long, not even a full week—that I'd like to take you, Ben, to either the ocean or the mountains tomorrow. We could leave early, and be back here for dinner. Just the two of us. What do you think?"

"Great!" Ben couldn't hide his initial excitement. "Yes," he added, making a thumbs-up sign, keeping it shielded in the crook of his arm. Mountains or ocean— it wouldn't be a difficult decision for him to make. If he picked the mountains, he knew they wouldn't be able to reach one of the peaks, but if he picked the ocean, he could and would swim in it, or at least dunk himself, no matter how cold the water was. And that would be a memorable event. He had never been in an ocean. The Pacific would be his first.

"What do you think?" Ian said, facing his sister.

Ben's mother hesitated. "I . . ."

There was a long pause. A dog barked far in the distance. Did it belong to the Deeters? Leaves rustled. Ian and Ben waited.

"Julie," said Ian, "a simple yes or no will do."

"I . . . really don't . . ."

"Trust you alone with him," said Ian.

"I didn't say that," Ben's mother replied sharply.

"You didn't have to."

Ben could feel his insides constrict to small, hard lumps.

Very quietly, Ben's mother said, "I kind of resent the fact that you didn't ask me first. I'm the parent. You sent the letter to Ben, not me. And now you ask this . . . out of the blue."

"God, Mom," said Ben, "I'm twelve years old."

"Ben, please." Ben didn't know her voice could sound so small, or strained.

Ian opened his mouth, as if to speak, and then his eyebrows snapped together and he turned his head to the side, saying nothing. He flipped the flashlight on and off repeatedly, the beam pointing straight down, illuminating a circle of dry grass.

Ben looked from his uncle to his mother several times; if only his eyes could knit them back together. But it seemed as though they had retreated to some separate, distant place, making Ben's task to turn the night around enormous, impossible.

All at once, Ben's mother and Ian walked away—
Ben's mother toward the house, Ian in the direction of
his studio.

The lights in the studio came on, and from across
the yard, Ben could hear the kitchen faucet running.
She's doing the dishes, he thought. He noticed his
mother's sandals near her chair, right where she had
tossed them off, and the napkin from Ian's shirt on
the ground beside them, a crumpled ball.

Ben stayed outside trying to decide what to do next,
and the stars just went on shining, unmindful, the
trees aloof.

Part Three

ANYWHERE

7

I COULD BE ANYWHERE, Ben thought. It didn't matter anymore that he was on vacation. He wanted to be home. He was mad at his mother. Right now, he should have been on his way to the ocean. Instead he was plodding upward through the sloping apple orchard, searching for the Deeters.

Ian was still in his studio, and for all Ben knew, that's where he had spent the night. Ben had heard hammering and the sound of a saw, both as he lay on the cot on the porch in the darkness trying to fall asleep, and as he woke at sunrise.

Nina had driven to Eugene for her weekly midwife appointment. She had asked Ben if he wanted to join her. "There's a great used bookstore next door and a bakery next to that with the best cinnamon rolls I've ever had. It'll take me an hour at the most." She was already in the car when she had asked him. The engine idled steadily. She tried to find a suitable radio station, settling on a classical one. Cellos swelled, louder, louder, until Nina turned the volume down. "I asked your mom—she said it was all right with her."

"No, thank you."

"Don't worry," she said. Her eyes met his, and held. "They'll be fine. I think they're a lot alike."

"What do you mean?" He touched the door handle.

"They're brooders. They think too much. Your uncle overanalyzes everything. And he's not very good at dealing with conflict," she told him, tinkering with a button on her shirt. "If something's difficult to talk about, I think he'd rather have all his teeth drilled without the benefit of novocaine than discuss it."

"Mom, too. Sometimes anyway. That's bad, huh?"

"Well, it makes them who they are. Everything gets complicated when you love someone." She smiled easily. "When I get back, we'll whip them both into shape," she said, reaching her hand out the window frame toward him. The gesture was somewhere between a wave and a pat. Then she took off slowly down the pocked dirt road, dust trailing behind the car like a little storm.

Ben's mother was baking chocolate-chip cookies, which was something she did with unrelenting drive, like a machine, whenever she was either extremely happy, extremely sad, or extremely angry. It was easy to eliminate happiness from the day's list of emotions.

"I'm going to walk over to the Deeters'," Ben had said. "Is that okay?"

"Sure." Ben's mother dropped a spoonful of dough onto a cookie sheet, then stood the spoon straight up in the bowl of dough. "Listen, I'm sorry about last night. . . ."

Ben shrugged. He could tell by her tight voice and grim expression that she was still upset. But he was, too. He couldn't escape the grip of anger; it kept him from directly addressing the issue of the trip to the ocean. "I left my radio tracking collar at home in Wisconsin, but don't worry. I'm not going very far."

Ben's mother didn't respond.

Cookies were stacked on the counter and heaped on cooling racks.

"Are you baking for the entire Northwest, or just the state?" Ben asked.

"I'll freeze most of them. I'm sure Ian and Nina can use them after the baby's born." She blew at her bangs. "Want a couple for your walk?"

"No." He did.

"How about a bag of them for the Deeters?"

"I'll skip it. I don't want to feel weighted down."

"Suit yourself."

He wanted to ask his mother why she would allow him to go to town with Nina, but not to the ocean with Ian. He could imagine her reply: "Driving to town and driving to the ocean are two entirely different things." And her tone would convey the underlying message: Come on, Ben, you're smarter than that.

"Ben?"

"Huh?"

"Nothing," she said, shaking her head.

She went back to her cookies, and after looking at her with a deliberately blank expression, he went out the door.

He had decided to look for the Deeters, just as a way to kill time, but then suddenly, fifteen minutes into his hike, he realized he truly wanted to see Lynnie. He walked with a purpose. The rows of identical trees revealed nothing, and after a while, the grassy corridors between the trees seemed mazelike. Row after row after row. Nothing. Nothing. Nothing. No Lynnie. Aware of his plunging disappointment, Ben grabbed a windfall apple from the ground and threw it with all his might. The apple arced high above the trees and disappeared into the vast expanse of green. He heard it drop through the branches and leaves and land with a thud.

"Hey! Who's there?"

"Someone's coming!"

Ben recognized Kale and Elka's voices and rushed toward them, ducking under low boughs and turning sideways to squeeze between branches. He could see them beyond the edge of the orchard, standing under a dead, gnarled tree that was taller than the others and set apart. Lynnie was lying on a beach towel in the spotty shade of the tree, reading. She picked up her head and acknowledged him with a smile and a wave.

She pressed a long blade of grass into her book to mark her place.

"Hi!" Ben shouted, running, closing the gap between him and the Deeters.

Kale and Elka moved toward Ben with their arms outstretched, as if they were guarding something. They stopped, firmly planted in protective stances. "Don't look at the tree," said Kale. His bony eyebrow ridges came to attention.

Impulsively Ben glanced up.

"I said *not* to look. Now you know our secret," Kale whined. His arms collapsed in defeat; his face crumpled.

"I don't know anything," said Ben.

"You have to promise not to tell," said Elka. A colorful paper chain was draped over her shoulders. Her fingers were wrapped around a red plastic stapler.

"You have to swear it," said Kale.

Ben had no idea what they were talking about.

Kale and Elka tugged on his shirt. "Promise! Promise!" they chanted.

"Okay, okay, I promise," he told them, chuckling.

Satisfied, the twins darted back to the base of the tree and busied themselves, and then Lynnie was right beside him. "I'm glad you came," she said. "I'm glad you didn't have something better to do with Ian and your mom."

"Well . . ." Ben began. "Yeah." He left it at that.

"I'll explain their big project to you, now that you're sworn to secrecy," she told him. She laughed gently and led him to the tree.

About five feet from the ground, the trunk of the tree split four ways. The divided stem cradled a huge gray tangle of brittle limbs and branches, some of which cascaded toward and touched the weedy grass. The whole thing looked like the nest of some prehistoric bird mashed down onto an odd, deformed pole.

"The tree's going to be their gift for Ian and Nina's baby," said Lynnie.

"The *tree*?" said Ben.

"The tree."

The closer Ben got, the more sense it made. He hadn't noticed from afar the ways in which the tree had been altered. Silver tabs from the tops of aluminum cans were hanging from the bottom branches on pieces of yarn. Additional tabs had been slipped directly onto the thinner twigs, like rings on the fingers of infants. In all, there must have been hundreds of the tabs, and when Ben moved his head a certain way, some of them glinted in the sun.

A bald, moonfaced baby doll was wedged firmly into the crook formed by a particularly twisty branch. The doll's doughy torso was made of cloth; the arms, legs, and head were plastic, the color of butterscotch.

Green and yellow pushpins held dozens of apple leaves from other trees to the craggy bark. Ben tried to see some pattern in the placement of the leaves but couldn't.

Lynnie picked at the point of one of the pinned-on leaves. "At first, they wanted to bring the tree back to life. They really thought they could. But it's been dead for a long time." She kept her voice quiet, so that the twins couldn't hear her, Ben guessed. But that didn't seem to be a problem; the twins were completely consumed, huddled over a beat-up metal cooler, making paper chains. "They dragged bottles of water out here every day in my grandma's rickety garden cart to try to revive the tree. When they finally gave up on that idea, they decided to decorate it."

"Why the tree?"

"Well," said Lynnie, moving over to where her beach towel lay, "partly because it's big. They have this notion that they want to give the baby a present that will be bigger than anyone else's present."

Ben grinned. "I think they'll win that contest."

"And my mom suggested they make something, rather than buy something."

Lynnie lifted a corner of the towel off the ground and pulled the towel behind her. Her book bumped along, then slid off the towel. Ben picked it up. Following her, he turned the book over in his hands. It was a copy of *Little Women* that appeared to have been read a thousand times. A small distance away, out of earshot of Kale and Elka, Lynnie found a suitable place—level ground, temporarily shaded by a cloud. She smoothed out the towel and sat. Ben sat, too, placing the book between them, facedown, the way he had found it.

"It's a neat tree," said Ben. "Looks ancient."

"The tree was planted even before my grandpa was born," said Lynnie. "It was the last of its kind in the whole orchard. It's called Seek No Further."

"*Seek No Further?* You're kidding."

"I'm serious."

"You mean, like McIntosh or Granny Smith?"

"Yep."

"No lie?"

"No lie."

"You mean, if I wanted an apple from this tree, I'd say, 'I'd like a Seek No Further, please'?"

Lynnie nodded. "*And* my grandpa says he kissed my grandma for the first time under this very tree. And that's why he won't cut it down. So it'll just stand here until it disintegrates."

"Hmm." Ben knew that if his mother were with them, she would say something about how sweet and lovely that bit of family history was.

"I tried to explain to Kale and Elka that you can't really give a dead old tree in an orchard to someone as a gift. Especially when it's our grandpa's, not theirs to give. But"—she looked over at them, and quickly looked back—"they're just weird little kids with weird ideas."

Maybe they'll grow up to give rooms as gifts, thought Ben.

"Seek No Further is probably the best apple name," said Lynnie, "but Northern Spy and Winter Banana aren't bad either."

"An apple called Banana—that's good," said Ben.

They laughed together.

And they went on talking. Lynnie talked a lot, and easily. Ben talked more than he ever had to a girl (which wasn't a lot), and with some effort. Not because he didn't want to, but because talking to a girl, alone, a girl he had only met the day before, a girl who was thirteen and whose belly button he had seen, was something new for him.

She told him that *Little Women* was her favorite book and that she'd first read it when she was nine and that she had reread it at least twice a year since then. She recited several lines from memory. He told her that the Tintin books were his favorites and that he owned nearly all of them and that even college students bought them at his parents' store.

She told him that she often wished she were an only child as he was and that on nights when she couldn't sleep she made up elaborate stories about her life as such, complete with exotic vacations, a canopy bed the size of a bus, indulgences galore. He told her that he sometimes wondered what it would be like to have a brother, and that when he was angry with his parents he thought it would be helpful to have someone else on his side to even things out.

"You'd probably end up fighting a lot," Lynnie said. "And why not a sister?"

Ben shrugged and ducked his head. "I don't know."

She told him that her mother had wanted to start home-schooling them, but Lynnie had talked her out of it, begging, because she couldn't bear the thought of not going to her regular school and being with other people, couldn't bear the thought of being stuck with Kale and Elka all year long. He told her that *he* had been home-schooled, for two years, kindergarten and first grade, and that he didn't remember it very clearly, but that his mother said he had wanted to be with his neighborhood friends badly, and so she finally let him go to the public school a few blocks away.

She told him that Ian had been giving her art lessons, and that he sometimes baby-sat Kale and Elka to practice being a father, and that he picked fruit for her parents when they were short on help. He didn't tell her anything about his uncle because he didn't know what to say.

Ben realized that he never just sat around and talked like this with his friends back home. They *did* things. They rode bikes or played basketball or went swimming. Talking seemed so natural to Lynnie; she was good at it. Maybe all girls were that way. Maybe that was one of the ways in which girls were different.

"What are you thinking?" Lynnie asked.

"Nothing." He zipped a glance at her.

"No, really. A few seconds ago, you had this look on your face like you'd just figured something out. Or something."

"I don't know."

After a moment's pause, Lynnie said, "I like you." She said it simply, as if she had said, "I'm hungry," and then she tightened her lips and blinked and hooked her hair behind her ears.

Ben looked straight ahead. Across the field, the leaves and fruit were suddenly limned in light and seemed ready to spring forth from the trees, to come right at him. Highlights were as sharp as glass, details as clear as those merely inches away.

"Our paper chains are ready!" shouted Kale, returning the world to normalcy just as quickly as it had become something else. "Help us put them on the tree!"

"Please!" yelled Elka.

"Should we?" Lynnie asked, rising.

"Sure," Ben replied, wondering if his hearing was reliable.

8

THE PAPER CHAINS hung from the lowest branches like strings of cursive writing. Ben wondered aloud about rain ruining the paper chains, but Lynnie said that it hardly ever rained during the summer, and there was no stopping Kale and Elka, regardless. When the last loop was securely attached, Kale and Elka decided it was time to put their nests on the tree, as well.

There were two nests, one from each of them, and they had been storing them in the silver cooler under the tree. Both of the nests were real, found in the orchard. Kale and Elka had filled them with small offerings.

Kale had chosen the following things for his nest: three fat rubber bands from his rubber band collection, a Hot Wheels tow truck ("I've got doubles of this one"), the lucky penny he had discovered two days earlier on the seat of his grandfather's tractor, and a tooth—one of his own baby teeth.

Elka fingered and counted each item in her nest: a tiny glass Christmas ornament ("Because Christmas is my favorite day"), a yellow button ("Because yellow is my favorite color"), a robin's egg she had kept on her dresser for over a year, and a lock of her hair tied with a yellow ribbon.

"The hair and the tooth are the best," said Kale.

"They're the most important," said Elka.

"Because they came from us," said Kale. He grinned to show the space where his tooth had been, a grin as wide as a jack-o'-lantern's.

"They really did," said Elka, sending her eyes up toward her bangs.

Picking the perfect spots for the nests was not easy. Kale and Elka circled the tree repeatedly. They jumped. They parted the branches within their reach. They stood on tiptoe, peering. They hopped onto the cooler, raised their arms, and blindly investigated the knot of dead branches over their heads.

Ben and Lynnie stood among the fallen twigs beneath the tree and watched without speaking. Ben wasn't really paying attention. His mind wandered. He scooped up a handful of twigs and broke them into the smallest possible pieces. He became acutely aware of how the day had taken a turn for the better. Thoughts of his mother and uncle had been swept clean away. Ben smiled. Lynnie smiled, too.

Finally Kale and Elka settled on a dark hollow halfway up the tree trunk. Side by side, they placed the nests into the hole. It was a tight fit, but the nests seemed safe, snug.

"It looks good, you guys," said Lynnie.

"Are you done with the tree?" asked Ben. "Or do you have other things to add?"

"We're done for right this minute," Kale answered. "But we've got lots more to do."

"We'll keep adding nice, beautiful things until the baby is born," said Elka. She grabbed Ben's hand and held it.

"Well, I think the nests are great," said Ben.

"If *you* had a nest for the baby, what would you put in it?" Elka asked Ben.

"Oh," he replied, "maybe a two-dollar bill and a stone or a shell from the ocean."

"What about the most important part?" Elka wanted to know. Her voice was so sincere, her eyes as clear as water. "Like my hair and Kale's tooth. The part from you."

"Hmm." His old blackened toenail came to mind, the one that had fallen off while playing basketball last year. He had saved it, hidden it away in the back of his desk drawer in his room. Something about it intrigued him, but he didn't want to mention it in case Lynnie thought it gross. "I don't know," he said. "I don't think I have anything."

"What about Icky Pee?" Kale asked.

"Icky Pee?" said Ben.

"Kale!" Lynnie whispered fiercely. "Be quiet!"

Ben's forehead wrinkled. He saw Lynnie curse Kale with her eyes. Elka's comment from dinner the night before raced back to him: *"Icky Pee is gone."* He knew, with a stab of insight, before the explanation came, that it was his missing finger they were talking about, and the knowing made him slip his left hand into his pocket.

Elka was still holding his right hand. She broke the grasp and turned his palm so it was open, facing her. One by one, she pointed to Ben's fingers, starting with his pinkie. "This is Icky Pee," she said. "And this is Penny Roo. And this is Mary Ossle. And this is Ollie Whistle. And this," she said, ending with his thumb, "is Big Tom Bobbilee." She couldn't help but smile. "Those are the names of the fingers. My grandma taught them to us." She grabbed his hand again, to hold it, but he wiggled free, pulled his hand away, and scratched his head.

"You don't have your other Icky Pee," Kale remarked.

"Do you know where it is?" Elka asked quietly.

"Can I see where it was?" asked Kale.

"What happened to it?" Elka whispered.

"You two—" Lynnie shook her head and exhaled noisily. "I . . ." She struggled for a moment. "I'm sorry," she said to Ben, blushing, looking at his shirt, not his eyes.

"It's okay," said Ben, pushing his other hand into his pocket, slowly, self-consciously.

"Will you show us?" Kale asked.

Lynnie said, "I'll take them home. It's almost lunch-time, anyway."

"No, wait," said Ben.

Normally, Kale and Elka's fascination with his missing finger wouldn't have bothered Ben (he might even have laughed about Icky Pee), but he could tell that Lynnie was embarrassed, and so he was embarrassed, too. His hands felt clammy and clumsy. If only he could distract Kale and Elka in some way, turn their attention from him to something better. Thinking fast, he looked at the tree. His eyes bounced about the dead wood and the decorations, lighting on nothing, until they picked out a fleck of green at the tree's highest point.

"Hey, look," Ben said loudly, nodding. "Look. At the top of the tree. I see green. Maybe the tree really *is* coming back to life."

Kale and Elka craned their necks. They took baby steps—to the side, forward—stopping when they caught the sliver of green in their sights. Their voices rang out. "There it is!" "It's a teeny weeny leaf!"

Soon the twins were hunched together, speaking in hushed tones. Ben couldn't make out much of what they were saying, but he did hear, "We should start watering it again," and "Maybe we could use some of Grandma's plant food."

A breeze sheared past, and Ben saw the little spot of green quiver. The green was not the green of a new leaf. It was too dark and shiny. He guessed it was a windblown piece of either a balloon or a plastic garbage bag that happened to be snagged on the tip of one of the tallest branches.

Ben and Lynnie went back to where Lynnie's beach towel was, but they remained standing. Silence fell between them for a few moments. The air was filled with so many noises, Ben thought, if you really listened. With his head dipped, chin to chest, Ben watched the rise and fall of his breathing.

Lynnie placed one foot flat against the inside of the opposite calf, balancing like some kind of waterbird. The foot slid down onto the other foot, then back onto the ground. She shifted her weight from one leg to the other. "They're really something," she said. "Sometimes I can't believe we're related."

"I didn't think they'd be that excited," said Ben, glancing up at the tree.

"You mean gullible," said Lynnie.

"Should I tell them?"

"No. They deserve it. They were so rude."

"Forget it."

Lynnie's head was bent and her shoulders were slightly stooped. "Was it the worst thing that ever happened to you?" Her eyebrows did a funny lift as she asked the question.

"No," Ben answered instantly. He was surprised by how emphatic he sounded. "I don't even remember it.

It happened when I was two." His hands were still in his pockets. They seemed to be boulders—big, impossibly heavy—attached to his arms. Gravity pulled at them. "Do you know how it happened?"

Lynnie regarded him with a quizzical tilt of her head and a questioning gaze. "I just met you yesterday. How would I know that?"

"I thought maybe Ian told you."

"No. I didn't even know Ian had a nephew until the day before you came."

The back of Ben's throat prickled. He took his hands out of his pockets, crossed his fingers, and traced tight figure-eights on his legs. He didn't want to betray his uncle, but he didn't want to be mysterious either, so he told the story of the accident. He finished by saying, "I guess my mom never really got over it, or something. I guess that's why I haven't seen him in so long."

A wave of understanding moved the planes of Lynnie's face. Her mouth opened, forming an *O*. "I bet that's why Ian doesn't want us in his studio, especially Kale and Elka."

"I guess." Ben wondered when Lynnie had noticed that his hand was different, but he was suddenly too shy to ask. And he was tired of talking about himself anyway. "What's the worst thing that ever happened to *you*?" he said.

"That's easy," Lynnie responded, the color in her

cheeks deepening. "A few years ago, I overheard my parents talking about money problems. How the orchards weren't doing as well as they should have been. How the truck needed to be repaired—again. How the bills were piling up. You know. So I had this great idea, which was really a stupid idea." She grimaced.

"What was it?"

"It was spring," Lynnie told him. "The blossoms were on the trees. And I have to say I love the blossoms even more than the fruit. At peak blossom time, the trees smell perfumey, and they look magical, like giant popcorn balls, drizzled with pink, growing on stems. Even when the blossoms are barely open, they're pretty. Then they remind me of the rosebuds on my grandma's bathrobe. A little bit of pink, a little bit of green."

While she was speaking, Lynnie had pushed her hair off the back of her neck, and gathered it into a ponytail. She twisted the ponytail and spooled it on her hand and wrist, then let it drop, her hair spilling freely over one shoulder. She sighed in a reflective way. "Anyway, because the trees looked so beautiful, I thought that if I cut some of the branches, I could sell them out on the highway to people in passing cars and make gobs of money for my parents."

Ben was nodding politely.

"I chose young trees because they were easier for me to reach, easier to cut. My dad—who loves the trees so much he must have radar—found me hacking away at my fourth tree with his old trusty lopping shears. I kind of ruined them—the trees. Not to mention decreasing the year's apple supply. He just stared right into me with these eyes that were surprised and then furious and then sad. I had filled a couple of buckets with water for the cut branches, and he kicked them across the grass and walked away. The branches shot out, petals dropped everywhere. My explanation sounded so lame when I heard myself blabbering the words as I ran after him. I mean, I knew better—I grew up on the farm. I must have been temporarily insane. I guess I just wanted the money for them *now*—I mean, *then*. You know what I mean. Anyway, he didn't say a thing to me for two whole days—not one single word. Later he told me he didn't want to try talking to me because he was afraid he would yell and scream, and he didn't want to do that."

The color in Lynnie's cheeks was so heightened now, Ben wanted to touch them to see if the red would rub off. She shook her head, as if by doing so, the incident would be jumbled and beyond recall. Her hair flew about, and Ben was close enough to smell her shampoo.

"Those two days were the worst days of my life," she said. "I was convinced he hated me, and that was unbearable. I kept rereading the chapter in *Little*

Women where Beth dies. I thought if I read the saddest thing I know, I'd feel better about me."

"Did it work?" was the weak question Ben managed to ask, because he felt he should say something.

"Not really." She looked past him, out at the prim and proper rows of trees and the hills and the outline of the mountains. "The chapter is called 'The Valley of the Shadow.' And so that's what I called this place. I still do, if I'm really sad about something, or when life is totally unfair."

The Valley of the Shadow. A good name, Ben thought, for the place where his mother and uncle were stuck. Where they had been stuck for years.

"Pretty dumb, huh?" said Lynnie. "It all sounds like something Kale and Elka would do."

"Your dad's not still mad about it, is he?" asked Ben.

"No. Not at all. Now he even jokes about it. But when I think about it, I feel hot all over, like I'm burning from the inside, like it happened yesterday."

A dull bell clanged in the distance precisely when Lynnie finished her sentence, putting an abrupt and ceremonious end to their conversation.

"That's my grandma's signal," Lynnie said, checking her watch. "It's time for lunch." She threw her beach towel around her shoulders and tied two of the frayed corners at her neck to make a cape. The towel strained at the knot. She clutched her book near her heart. "Do you want to walk together? Till the twisty path to Ian's?"

"Sure." Ben had already become familiar enough with the land to know exactly where Lynnie meant.

"Why don't you look for us later? Now you know where we'll be."

"Okay. I'll see what's going on at my uncle's."

"I can pay you then. You know, your baby-sitting money."

"You don't have to."

"Hey," said Lynnie, repositioning the towel, "I still don't know what *your* worst thing is."

Ben shrugged. "If I think of it, I'll let you know."

At the tree, Lynnie hurried the twins along, and then the four of them set out together. Kale and Elka were still buzzing about the leaf. They made Ben renew his vow of silence concerning the tree, after which Ben whispered to Lynnie, "Should we tell them now?"

"Let's not," Lynnie whispered in reply. "It'll keep them occupied for a while." And five minutes later, as they went their separate ways, Lynnie added, "Don't worry, Ben. The wind'll just take care of it anyway."

Ben stepped onto the sheltered path to a flurry of birds' wings. With the midday sun beating down through the filter of leaves, he returned to his uncle's house.

9

THE CAR WAS BACK, parked in its space, which meant that Nina was home from the midwife. And yet, on the porch, Ben felt a twinge of dread. Ever so slowly, he turned the doorknob. What would he find? Rooms of silence? A bitter argument?

What he did find, in the living room, confused him, and frightened him at first. One end of an ironing board was propped on the seat of the couch, and Nina was lying on the board, her knees bent gently up toward her swollen belly, her head near the floor, supported by a bed pillow. Beside her, Ben's mother knelt, stroking Nina's hair with one hand; in her other hand she held a piece of paper. Ian, it appeared to Ben, was lightly pressing the earphones from a portable CD player to Nina's lower abdomen, directly to her skin. Her pants were pulled down, a wreath of folds around the tops of her thighs.

Feeling as if he were just a trace of himself, Ben hung in the doorway, watching. Was Nina having the baby right here? he wondered. Right now? Were they trying to stop the baby from spilling out? And was that why Nina's head was down and the rest of her body elevated? Ben's presence went unnoticed until he cleared his throat and blurted, "What's going on? Is everyone all right?"

"Oh, Ben—" his mother said, her head jerking in an arc toward the sound of his voice. "Everything's fine." She rose and came to him.

"Hello, Ben," Nina breathed, without changing her position on the board.

"Hey, Ben," said Ian. "This must look very odd to you."

Ben's mother peered at the clock on the mantle across the room. "Time's up," she said.

Nina wiggled the elastic waistband on her light, stretchy pants over the bulge that was her baby. With a bit of difficulty, Ian helped her off the ironing board and onto her feet. "I don't think it worked," she said.

"Be patient," said Ian. "This was our first attempt."

Somewhat urgently, Ben said, "Would someone please tell me what's happening?"

"The baby is breech," said his mother.

When he heard the word *breech*, Ben immediately thought: The baby has some rare disease. He learned, however, that it meant that the baby was in a position inside Nina that was not desirable for an easy birth. The baby was sitting cross-legged, buttocks down.

"We were trying to turn the baby," Ian explained. "Lying on the ironing board will, with luck, encourage the baby to float into a good position. Head down."

Ben's mother flipped and straightened the sheet of paper she had been holding so that Ben could see it. On it were illustrations showing the different types of breech presentation, and an illustration of a woman lying on an ironing board with arrows indicating the direction in which the baby should rotate.

"How do you know that the baby's the wrong way?" Ben asked.

"The midwife suspected it right away, just by feeling my belly," said Nina. "Then she sent me to a clinic with an ultrasound machine. To verify her suspicion. They gave me a copy of the scan. Look." She pulled a small, flimsy piece of paper out of her pocket and handed it to Ben. "This is our baby."

It was a ghostly image, white on black, like scratches of light coming through a dark cloth. Although grainy, it was most definitely the picture of a baby. A baby so compact, so round, a baby filling its space so completely, Ben doubted it could ever reverse itself. This is my cousin, he thought. My wrong-way-round cousin.

Ben gave the photograph back to Nina, saying, "But everything's okay, right?"

Nina told him that only three to four percent of the time babies were breech, and that it could make for a riskier birth, but in most cases, one way or another, breech births turned out well.

"Ours will be a great birth," Ian announced rather

loudly. He pecked Nina's cheek, and did the same to Ben's mother.

"Mmm-hmm," Ben's mother murmured, nodding. "It will."

"Do you know if it's a boy or girl?" Ben asked Nina.

"No," she answered, "I don't. I'm sure I could have found out this morning, but I want it to be a surprise."

During lunch, Ben finally got around to asking Ian what he had been doing with the CD earphones.

"It's just another way to help turn the baby. Apparently a fetus can hear very well at this point, so maybe it'll move its head down to hear the music better." Ian bunched up his shoulders.

"What kind of music were you playing?" asked Ben.

"The midwife said to try Bach," Nina replied.

Ben laughed. He hadn't meant to; the laugh had just slipped out.

"I agree," said Ian. "It all sounds very funny."

"If you think that's funny," said Nina, working at a smile for Ben's benefit, "you'll appreciate this: Tonight, when's it's dark, your uncle or mom—or you, if you'd like—will hold a flashlight against me and draw it slowly down my belly. The light may attract the baby, causing the baby to move where we want it to."

Admittedly, Ben knew very little about babies. To him, they had always been mysterious creatures, helpless lumps, and so it seemed strange to imagine his cousin-to-be—still separated by a barrier of skin and muscle—listening to Bach or being able to follow the path of a light. He laughed once more.

No one ate very much, Ben noticed, and when they were finished, Ian said, "I'm happy we're all together."

Ben went to the cot on the porch to digest all the information he had received. He lay on his stomach and tucked his hands under the pillow. He was puzzled. If everything was supposedly fine, why were Nina's eyes rimmed in pink? He had seen her fingers tremble on her lap as he left the kitchen, and he had seen the wads of tissues crowding her pocket. And why were his mother and Ian suddenly acting as if last night had never happened? There was such an obvious change in their behavior, like a sudden shift in the weather, and that, Ben guessed, meant that something more serious was going on.

He stayed in or near the house all afternoon, sorting things out, trying to make sense of the situation. Most of the time, the three adults were in the kitchen nursing mugs of tea and coffee. They paged through books about pregnancy—index hopping and reading short passages aloud. Ben sensed an effort on their part to be upbeat.

For a while, he sat outside, on a rock, sketching. And for a while, he lost himself to his art. He drew a small section of grass as detailed as he possibly could, being mindful of shadow, light, texture. Then he worked on a rendering of the tree line, dense and dark, and the sunshine above it, and the curtain of clouds that had moved in above that. Accidentally, he smudged the drawing with his arm, but he liked the effect—perfect for clouds—and so he used his fingers as tools and the hem of his T-shirt, too, rubbing the pencil marks into the paper with varying amounts of pressure.

He needed to use the bathroom, but to avoid questions such as "What are you doing?" or "How are you?" he decided to stay outside and use the bushes behind the storage shed instead. He walked along the length of the house en route, and as he slipped around the far corner, he nearly collided with Nina.

Nina gasped. She had been crying. "Caught me," she said. She turned away and waited a moment, as if she were recovering her dignity, before she faced him and spoke again. "I'm sorry."

"That's okay," Ben squeaked. "*I'm* sorry."

"I just needed to be outside," she said.

Ben nodded.

"It's silly to be crying," she said. "I know that."

Ben pushed his shoulder against the house; his shirt sleeve caught on one of the rough cedar shingles.

Nina said, "My best friend, Nancy—we've been friends since we were six—was pregnant, too. She was due about eight weeks ago. Her baby was breech, like mine." She lowered her eyes and concentrated on her thumbnail. "During the birth there was a complication with the umbilical cord—do you know what that is?"

"Yeah."

"Of course you do, you're twelve," she said, shaking her head. "Anyway, because the baby was breech, there was a problem with the cord...and the baby died." Her voice had thinned to a thread.

Hearing this, Ben stood straighter and offered her a rueful smile. There was absolutely nothing he could say.

"I know that every situation is different," Nina said, "but finding out that my baby is breech brought back all the sadness about my friend's baby, but in a whole new way. And it reminded me that something awful— the worst—could happen. To me. To us," she added, looking downward.

"Yeah." He bit his lip.

"But," Nina said, a kink in her eyebrow, "on a happier note, my terrible morning smoothed things between Ian and your mom." She looked directly at him. "Your mom has been very kind to me. Reassuring. And you are very kind, too, you know."

Ben blushed and frowned. His frown was like a twitch.

"I didn't mean to embarrass you." Nina's voice perked up. "Do you know what? I'm making it my mission to turn this baby." She stuck her chin out as if to punctuate her statement.

"How will you know if it happens?"

"The midwife said that some women feel it very

strongly, and others have it happen without feeling it at all. They'll check me next week," she added.

"The head's supposed to be down, right?" said Ben.

"Right."

"So upside down is really right side up?"

"I hadn't thought about it like that before, but, yes, upside down *is* right side up."

They laughed silently.

"Say that ten times fast," Nina joked. She motioned with her hand for him to come along.

Forgetting about his sketchbook and his need to pee, Ben fell into step with Nina. They entered the house.

"Let's take advantage of their truce," Nina whispered. "Do you like to play cards?"

≈   ≈

They played hearts and spades. Ben, his mother, Ian, and Nina. They played gin and poker. They played for hours, not even stopping for a real dinner, but eating pretzels, and peanut-butter-and-jelly sandwiches slapped together quickly between games. They played as the shadows lengthened and darkness collected in the valley, among the trees, in the house.

Not long after, with great interest, Ben watched Ian drag a flashlight slowly, slowly down Nina's white moon-belly while she lay on the ironing board. It was the only light in the black room, and it looked red against her skin when it leaked out from the lip of the flashlight. Rather than music, this time Ian tried to coax the baby with his voice. He spoke clearly, sweetly.

"Come on, baby," he said. "Come down here. Down here to Papa. I'm so excited to meet you. We've only got about a month to go. Your aunt, Julie, and your cousin, Ben, are here now. Let's call this their first visit with you. Come on, baby. Turn around. You can do it. Come to Papa. . . ."

Ben's mother held the flashlight when Ian's arm fell asleep. Ben didn't want to. But he inched closer and closer until the four of them were like one small planet floating in an endless night sky. No one and nothing else existed. They were all alone in the universe. Together.

Part Four

NOWHERE

10

One. Two. Three. Ben was seeing how many steps he could take with his eyes closed. If I make it to twenty-five, he thought, Mom and Uncle Ian will stay friends and the baby will turn around before we go home. He was on his fifth attempt. *Six. Seven. Eight.* His father had called as they were eating breakfast that morning, and although Ben didn't talk very long or tell about everything that was happening, it was good to hear his father's voice. Happy from the telephone call and full from breakfast, he cautiously traced the edge of the orchard toward the tree to see if Lynnie and the twins were there. *Ten. Eleven. Twelve.* A branch poked his shoulder; he swiveled but kept going, his eyelids clamped down. He had left his mother, aunt, and uncle in the field between the house and the studio, shovels in hand, breaking up grass and weeds, forming a circle of freshly turned dirt—a garden for the baby. Nina wanted to fill it completely with bulbs so that it would be bursting with color and life in the spring. Their conversation as they worked had been as constant as the birdsong. *Sixteen. Seven-*

tee— His foot landed in a hole and he opened his eyes. He'd give it one more try.

One. Two. Three. Four. Five. Six. When he first heard the noise, it was soft and muffled. He might not even have noticed it at this point if his eyes hadn't been closed. By shutting off one sense, he had sharpened his others. He cocked an ear. The noise grew. *Thirteen. Fourteen. Fifteen.* He stopped. He could feel the noise throughout his entire body like another pulse. His eyes flew open and he ran to the sound.

An old man was chopping at the tree—*the* tree— with an ax, in a steady rhythm like a mechanical toy. At a safe distance, Lynnie was picking things off the ground and plucking things from the fallen branches and putting them into the old metal cooler. The twins were nowhere to be seen.

The bulk of the tree came crashing down. By the time Ben reached it, the stump was all that was left standing. The stump rose out of the ground, pointy and cavernous as a big rotten tooth. Limbs and branches were strewn about. Heaps of them. The old man had moved over and was chopping at the largest limbs, one of which was so crumbly the ax could barely be heard. Another was so brittle it cracked and snapped upon impact. The silver tabs and pieces of the paper chains dangled here and there among the debris. Ben realized these were the things Lynnie was gathering.

Ben was standing in Lynnie's shadow before she saw

him. "What's going on?" he asked. "Who is that? What is he *doing*?"

"Ben—hi." Lynnie looked over to the old man and looked back. "That's my grandpa," she said weakly. She seemed distracted. She dropped a handful of tabs into the cooler, then knit her fingers together at her waist. A second later, she unlaced her fingers and folded her arms across her chest. "Last night," she said in a hushed voice, "Kale ran off and tried to climb to the very top of the tree to get a better look at the leaf." Her face curdled when she said *leaf.* "The branches are so old and dead they gave way and he fell. Probably twenty feet. His head hit the cooler. He got a concussion, and he broke his arm and his leg. He's all scratched and cut up, too. He got twenty-two stitches."

"Oh, God," Ben whispered. Fear flicked inside his rib cage. He had so many questions, he didn't know where to start. "How . . . who . . . found him?"

"I was there," said Lynnie. "It was dinnertime. We had been at the tree, and we were partway home, when he just took off on me. It was hard because I had to keep an eye on Elka and go get Kale, too. By the time I caught up with him, he was already in the tree.

"I asked him what he was doing, and he said, 'I want to see the leaf,' and he just kept climbing like a squirrel or a monkey or something. I yelled that it wasn't real, but he didn't listen. I said it again, and he still didn't pay attention. I guess he wanted to see for himself. And then one of the limbs cracked and broke and he fell, screaming. I can still hear the branches snapping, and his head slamming against the cooler."

Lynnie squeezed her eyes shut, and cringed. "He was really bleeding. See—there's even some on the grass," she said, casting her eyes to the ground to spots of dried blood. "I ran to get my dad. He drove my grandpa's car to the tree and wrapped Kale in his jacket and lifted him into the car like a baby. He drove to the hospital—" She stopped abruptly, as if she had run out of words or lost her concentration. She turned toward her grandfather, briefly. "My grandpa says it's his fault for not cutting the tree down a long time ago."

Ben remembered the story Lynnie had told of her grandparents kissing for the first time beneath the tree. He remembered her saying her grandfather had left the dead tree standing for that reason. A nostalgic monument.

Lynnie said, "He keeps apologizing to my parents and Kale. And that's not like my grandpa. At all."

Ben's thoughts were a turmoil.

"I'm collecting Kale and Elka's stuff," Lynnie explained. "They're all upset about their gift being ruined."

In a weighted silence, Ben helped Lynnie gather the

tabs and the bits of the paper chains. The baby doll that had been wedged into a crook and the nests were already in the cooler. Everything seemed inert, slowed down, even the air.

All of a sudden, Ben felt pressure on his shoulder. It was Lynnie's grandfather's hand. "Hello," said the voice that went with the hand. "You must be Ian's nephew."

Ben nodded. "I'm Ben."

"Call me Joe," said Lynnie's grandfather. Sweat dripped down his tanned, wrinkled, stricken face. He wore a baseball cap, pulled low to shield his eyes. Snow white wings of hair shot out from under the cap and covered his ears. His legs and arms were skinny as poles. "That's that," he said. "I'll clean this up later. I'm going back to the barn, sweetie." He kissed Lynnie's head. "Seek no further," he muttered, scanning the messy landscape. He took one last swipe with his ax at a hill of branches.

When her grandfather was out of sight, Lynnie removed something small from her pocket, something so small her fingers concealed it easily. "I found this." She opened her hand. "This morning."

Ben knew what it was instantly. "The leaf," he said, staring. It was just a thin scrap of green plastic with rippled edges. No more, no less.

"It was stuck on a branch," said Lynnie. She twirled it and twirled it and twirled it.

"How *is* Kale?" Ben asked. "I mean, he's going to be okay."

"Yeah, but last night I was so scared. Right after he fell, he said he couldn't see anything for about a minute, and I thought he was blind. My mom kept waking him up during the night to make sure he was conscious, and she checked his eyes with a flashlight to make sure the pupils were equal in size. He's got one cut by his eye that the doctor says will leave a scar. Actually, Kale's excited about *that*."

"It's my fault," they both said at exactly the same moment after a short pause.

"No, mine," said Lynnie. "You wanted to tell them it wasn't real. I asked you not to."

"But it was my idea in the first place."

"Yeah, but you were just distracting them from . . . talking about your finger."

"We have to tell your grandpa and your parents," Ben said grimly. "Explain everything."

"I already did," Lynnie said.

"And?"

"And my grandpa still thinks it's his fault. And my mom and dad said something like: 'Kale is Kale,' and 'You didn't make him climb the tree,' and 'Accidents happen.' And it doesn't matter what I say to Kale—he's furious that we tricked him. Elka, too."

Ben nodded.

"Do you want this?" Lynnie asked, holding up the

green plastic snippet between her thumb and index finger.

Ben shook his head no.

"Me neither." She took a long breath and blew hard. The piece of plastic rose and looped through the air like a dark, crazy butterfly, then dropped to the ground. "Will you help me carry the cooler to the house? If I do it myself, I'll have to drag it like a mule would."

"Sure."

They each grabbed a handle and set out. It wasn't a heavy load by any means, but because Ben was taller and took bigger steps, the cooler banged into their legs every few feet, making it an awkward trip. They finally found a rhythm and even began to swing the cooler in arcs that grew progressively larger.

"Do you think Kale will forgive us?" Ben asked.

"I don't know," Lynnie replied. "Eventually. Maybe. We'll see."

≈   ≈

Lynnie's house was old and boxy and pigeon gray with a steep green roof like a pointed hat. Toys of all kinds were scattered about the patchy yard. Scruffy cats— Ben counted five—came out to greet Lynnie from behind or under the temporary shelter of buckets, crates, and an open umbrella.

"They're wild," said Lynnie. "Barn cats. But I feed them."

The cats wove in and out of Lynnie's legs, purring. If the cats had been trailing rope, Lynnie's ankles would have been bound together in a tangle.

Lynnie lost her grip on the handle. It slipped out of her hand, her end of the cooler hit the stone slab on which she and Ben were standing, and the cats shot off in all directions.

"Do you need help?" floated a calm voice from within the darkness of the house.

"No, Grandma," Lynnie called, picking up her handle. "We've got it under control."

The front door sprang open, as if by magic. But really it was Lynnie's grandmother who had thrust the door open and held it as Ben and Lynnie squeezed through. The grandmother's long, pale arm was stretched across the screen. The fingers on her spidery hand were spread widely, a five-point star. "Rest a minute," she said.

Ben and Lynnie gently lowered the cooler onto the entryway floor. Ben thought that Lynnie's grandmother looked like a female version of her grandfather. They had similar hair, similar builds, and the same icy blue eyes. More like brother and sister, he thought, than husband and wife.

"Grandma, this is Ben, Ian's nephew," said Lynnie. She continued the introduction, "Ben—my grandma.

She goes with the grandpa you just met. They live across the way, but she's staying here today in case Kale needs anything. My mom and dad are picking."

"Hello, Ben. Nice to meet you."

"Hi. Me, too," said Ben.

"I'm glad your paths crossed this morning," said Lynnie's grandmother. "I pictured Lynnie lugging that chest alone through the orchards and fields." She turned to her granddaughter. "Your brother really wants to have that thing upstairs."

"I'm waiting," Kale yelled from above.

"Waiting," Elka echoed.

"Coming," Lynnie shouted.

The cooler bumped against walls, the railing, and the steps as they ascended the narrow, twisty staircase.

"First door on the left," Lynnie directed.

"King Kale, your loyal servants have arrived with your treasure chest," Ben announced from the hall.

"It's mine, too," Elka said, popping out from behind the door.

Ben and Lynnie entered Kale's room.

The shock of seeing Kale caused Ben's knees to slacken, his cheeks to burn. Kale's small pink face was stitched like a rag doll's and was uneven, swollen in places as if stuffing had bunched up inside. The longest cut on his face was dangerously near his right eye, and Ben sighed, relieved that the eye hadn't been poked out. The cast on Kale's arm was a rigid capital L lying on its back; the cast on his leg and foot added so much bulk that his other leg seemed as thin and fragile as an icicle. He sat in bed, propped up on a mountain of pillows. Broken.

"I'm sorry," said Ben. "I'm so sorry."

"I'm mad at you guys," Kale said sternly. His eyes flashed, then roved like searchlights. "You tricked us."

"You did," said Elka, leaning into the footboard of Kale's bed. One of her legs and one of her forearms were wrapped in towels that were secured with rubber bands—imitations of Kale's casts. As a sympathetic gesture, she limped around the room, holding her arm frozen at a right angle. She returned to the bed and clumsily scooted up onto the mattress. She adjusted her towels and rubber bands.

Without realizing it, Ben had let go of the cooler (Lynnie had, too). It sat in the middle of the room, and Ben had worked his way over to the window. "I didn't mean it. To trick you. Or for you to get hurt."

Kale wiggled the toes on his uninjured foot.

"It's hard to wash with casts on," Elka stated matter-of-factly, snapping her rubber bands. "And it itches underneath sometimes."

Ben wished he could shuck his skin off, change his insides, too. Start this trip all over. He pinched the bridge of his nose. "Is there something I can do to make it up to you?"

"*We*," said Lynnie. "Something *we* can do . . ."

112

Kale and Elka exchanged a glance and shrugged. "Maybe," Kale replied, considering. "Maybe, if you think of a new gift, I'll forgive you. But it's got to be better than the tree, or at least as good. And it's got to be big. *Like* a tree. Or a house," he added, regaining some of his spark, but only for a second. He wiggled his toes again.

"Okay," said Ben. "We'll think of something." He wanted to leave. He wanted to be outside. The room seemed so small, and growing smaller, and everywhere he looked was Kale with his grave, sewn-up face.

Minutes later, Ben and Lynnie were settled on the steps of the porch, and the wide outdoors rolled on forever. No walls, no ceiling. "We *will* think of something," Ben told Lynnie, although he hadn't a clue as to what that something might be.

11

Since Ben and his mother would be returning to Wisconsin in just two days, Ben knew there was very little time to come up with a gift that would be satisfactory to Kale. So that first morning after Kale's accident, Ben and Lynnie went right to work. Although they brainstormed for hours, all their ideas were flawed. They were either too easy—a banner made from a bedsheet and hung from Ian's studio; or too grand—the word BABY spelled out by a skywriter in letters the size of clouds for everyone to see. (How would they ever find a skywriter? Where? And how could they afford one, even if they located one?)

Ben's idea to plant a young apple tree in honor of the baby struck him as perfect. Not Lynnie. She convinced Ben that Kale would never go for it. It wouldn't be a big gift *now*, she pointed out; it would take years to grow big. He would feel as though he were being tricked again.

They both tried to keep Kale's words in mind: ". . . it's got to be big. *Like* a tree. Or a house." And so a tree house seemed obvious and logical. But only momentarily. Considering the circumstances, the nature of Kale's accident, they soon decided that a tree house was completely wrong, even ironic.

"Another Valley of the Shadow day," Lynnie said flatly. She arched her fingertips together, her elbows on her knees.

"Yeah," replied Ben. "I know what you mean." He was tired of thinking. His head hurt.

They were still on the porch. The sun had shifted. Now sunlight—fragmented by the trees—dappled their legs, their shoes, their heads.

"I just thought of something weird," said Lynnie.

"What?" said Ben.

"It's too weird to say."

"Go ahead. You can say it."

"Are you sure?"

"Yeah."

"Okay, but remember, it's weird." Lynnie was quiet for a long time, and then she said, "I was thinking again how if you asked me, I'd say that Kale's accident was my fault, and you'd say it was your fault. Grandpa would say it's his. And it's not like there's one right answer. And—this is the weird part—maybe it's the same thing with your hand. Maybe it wasn't only Ian's fault. Maybe . . . I mean, who knows? I mean, you'll never really know, it was so long ago." She held a finger to her lips, pondering. "Dumb thought," she added, as if to dismiss everything she had just said.

Ben took this in. He lifted his head and squinted

directly at the sun. This possibility had never occurred to him before. Heat seeped through his eyelids. When he lowered his head, his expression read: Who cares? Although he did care, of course. And then, all at once, he leaped off the porch. "I should go check in with my family," he said.

"Okay, but come back as soon as possible," said Lynnie, rising from what looked like a comfortable, miserable slouch and grabbing onto the porch railing.

"Okay," replied Ben in a surprisingly deep voice.

"Okay," said Lynnie, imitating Ben, making a kind of a joke.

"Okay," Ben repeated, smiling.

"Okay."

"Okay."

They continued their exchange—calling, calling, like two unusual birds—until Ben was lost to the trees and neither could see nor hear the other.

≈   ≈

Word of Kale's mishap had traveled, and Ian and Nina asked Ben how Kale looked, how he seemed. Ben answered their questions and told what he knew, except for the part about the green plastic leaf. He didn't lie; he just didn't fill in each and every detail.

Ben intended to return to Lynnie's right after lunch, but he wasn't the only one with a plan.

"Since we won't be making it to the ocean or the

mountains," said Ian, "how about a trip to the post office? It's not exactly in the same category, I admit."

Because Ben's mother was clearly within earshot and didn't react, Ben assumed that she must have already granted permission. "Yes," he said.

"Great," said Ian.

They said good-bye and drove away.

Stones hit the bottom of the car and dust rose in its wake until they reached the highway. Then they picked up speed. Traffic was light. Ben looked at everything around him. The somber hills. The mountain peaks—far off, wrinkled, like tissue paper glued to the sky. Sheep. The occasional logging truck. Stands of fir trees that surely were older than any person he had ever met.

"Kale is a funny kid," said Ian. "A good kid. I'm glad nothing more serious happened. I picture him scaling Everest someday, or sailing around the world solo. It's interesting how you can tell already what he'll be like as an adult. It's not so obvious with everyone. Some people . . . with some people it's harder to know."

Ben laughed, a half laugh. It was comforting to hear someone talk about Kale without dwelling on the accident.

"The last time I saw *you*," said Ian, "you were too little for me to know very well. I never saw you enough."

"Yeah."

"I've been trying to spend more time with the Dee-ters, to learn about kids. Practice for being a parent."

Ben nodded.

They passed a sign that read OCEAN BEACHES. The sign had an arrow indicating a turn to the left, but no indication as to how many miles separated them from the sea. Ben guessed one hundred.

"The, uh, the reason," Ian said stiffly, "*one* of the reasons I invited you for this visit was so that I could see you before we have the baby." He swallowed, and his Adam's apple bobbed. It looked as if a large grape were lodged inside his throat. "I needed to know that you were okay, that I hadn't ruined your life."

"You didn't," Ben said, surprised. He rolled his window up and down, changing the air inside the car. "Really."

Ian was wearing sunglasses. For the most part, he kept his head fixed straight ahead, his eyes pinned to the road. "I'm sorry," he said, his eyes darting to the side.

"It's okay," said Ben. "No problem." He continued to play with the window. "You know, I heard that we don't really need our pinkies anyway. And that maybe in a couple hundred years or so, people won't even be born with them. We'll lose them, evolutionarily. An anthropologist said so on National Public Radio, so it must be true."

Ian chuckled.

"I don't just sit around and listen to NPR," Ben explained. "Mom and Dad have it on in the bookstore. That's where I heard it."

Ian sighed an enormous sigh, then smiled. He was gripping the steering wheel with one hand and tapping it with the other. "You are one of the most okay people I've ever known." He sighed again. Dark trees sped by. "After the accident," he said, "I vowed I'd never have kids of my own. I was afraid of them, couldn't even hold one. So when I found out that Nina was going to have a baby, I panicked. In April, I took off for a couple of weeks to be alone, to think. I was so . . . I don't know—worried, I guess. Worried about what kind of parent I'd be, because of what I'd done to you."

It was almost as if Ian were talking to himself.

"I camped up in the mountains," Ian continued, "seeing how little I could get by on. Bread, cheese, water, fruit. And one very cold, starry night, I decided I wanted to see you. I decided that that was what it would take. . . ."

Ben didn't know how to respond. It felt odd to be confided in.

Ian said, "Seeing you has allowed me to begin again."

Ben pushed his knees against the glove compartment and sank into his seat. He coughed once. After a minute or two, he said, "So Aunt Nina knows all about my hand?"

"Of course."

"Does Mom know what you just told me?"

"No. I suppose she thinks this trip— Actually, I don't know what she thinks."

"Are you going to tell her?"

Ian shook his head. "Not necessary. Unless you want to. And it's fine with me if you do."

"Nah." It would be their secret. Ben turned to his uncle and started to ask something. "Will you—" but couldn't finish.

"You can ask me."

"Will you tell me about the accident?"

Something out the window, something unseen to Ben, seemed to catch Ian's attention. "I suspect you've heard it all before," he said. "I still don't really know how it happened. It happened so fast. I was baby-sitting you at my house, and I had given you a little chair I had built and you were very excited about it, as I remember. But the legs were too long. And uneven. I told you I'd fix the chair as soon as your mom came to pick you up. She was late and you wanted your chair and so I took you down to my basement workshop. . . . I was a stupid, stupid—" He stopped himself. With the heels of his hands guiding the steering wheel, he raised his fingers in a gesture that said halt, enough.

He had said the words quickly, but Ben had heard them: "She was late . . ."

"I understand why your mom was mad at me," said Ian, but Ben was barely listening, now. ". . . the misery I'm responsible for."

They drove and drove. Neither spoke. Ian turned off the highway, and they threaded through a small town. The bubble of silence between them grew. Ian finally pierced it by announcing, "Here's the post office."

The post office was a yellow brick cube, so small it seemed more like a playhouse than an official government building. Ian drew the car up to a curbside mailbox in front of it. He retrieved an envelope from behind the sun visor. Ben could tell that it was a credit-card payment, nothing more important than that. Ben also noticed the stamp, for some reason, as the envelope floated through the air in Ian's hand. The stamp had a peach on it. Which, for a moment, reminded him of Lynnie. And Kale. And the problem of the gift.

Ian dropped the envelope into the mailbox. He steered the car around, and they started back.

≈　≈

She was late.

Was it true? He believed what he had heard, and why not? Ian had said these three particular words so plainly, without any hesitation.

What would have happened all those years ago if his mother hadn't been late? And how late had she been? Five minutes? A half hour?

Maybe nothing would have happened—no accident. Or maybe something worse. Or maybe nothing would have happened differently. There was no way to tell, no reason to speculate. One thing always leads to another, he thought.

He didn't think he could ask her about it. He pictured her crying or becoming silent or hating Ian more than ever. All the progress they had made wasted.

He could feel the pressure mounting behind his eyes. His throat closed over.

"Does the radio work?" Ben asked, blinking. He remembered Nina using it.

"Yeah. Sure," said Ian. "Here." He clicked the radio on. The dial was set on a classical station. "The choice is yours."

Ben flipped the knob around until he found something he liked. He turned the volume up a bit. Up a bit more. Music filled the car all the way back to the house.

12

In one smooth motion, Ian took his sunglasses off and pushed them onto the top of the dashboard. "Thank you, Ben," he said. He turned the engine off and struggled for a moment to remove the key from the ignition switch.

"You're welcome," Ben replied, shrugging.

"We'll do the ocean *and* the mountains next time," Ian told him. "Now that we can check the post office off our list." He smiled; lines fanned out from the corners of his eyes.

Standing outdoors in the strip of shadow beside the car, Ian extended his right hand. Ben took it in his and shook it firmly. And then, Ian reached out with his left hand. Caught unawares, Ben hesitated at first, then did the same. He couldn't remember ever having used his left hand to shake with before. It felt unfamiliar. The grasp broken, Ben curled his fingers tightly against his palms.

"Hey," said Ian, "I almost forgot. You *are* a good artist. Your mother wasn't just bragging."

"What do you mean?" Ben asked at once, his forehead creased.

"I found your sketchbook outside this morning."

"Oh, God," said Ben. "I forgot about it." He hoped his uncle didn't think he was ungrateful.

"It was a little damp from the dew. I put it in my studio." Ian added, "I didn't mean to snoop, but it was open to a wonderful drawing of the tree line and some clouds. Come on, I'll give it back to you."

In the studio, Ben felt a rush of pride as he looked at the sketchbook open in front of them on Ian's workbench. The drawing *was* good. Ian flipped through the pages. "This is nice, too," he commented, pointing to the detailed section of grass Ben had done right outside the house. "And this." Now the sketchbook was open to a quick drawing of a gnarled apple tree. "You've captured it so well, and with very few lines. That's not an easy thing to do. And you already know how to vary the weight of the line. Some people never learn that."

Ben could see Ian's sketchbooks on the large bookshelf on the far wall. There were dozens and dozens of them, one lined up next to the other in perfectly ordered rows. He started counting them, but it was too difficult; they were nearly all the same size and color, and became a blur.

"You can look at them if you want to," said Ian.

"Really?" said Ben.

Ian nodded. "Let me help you."

They looked at the sketchbooks together, taking random armfuls of them down from the shelf to the workbench and leaning over them, turning the pages.

"Wow," said Ben. "You're a good drawer. The best I've ever seen. Even better than Ms. Temple, my last year's art teacher."

"Thanks."

One book was filled with drawings of leaves, nothing else. Another with only stones and rocks. Several were filled with sketches of furniture—tables, chests, stools, chairs. Ben found the two sketchbooks Ian had told him about previously, the ones that were entirely devoted to bark. In Ben's favorite sketchbook, page after page was covered with scenes of New York City. Tall buildings, crushes of people, pigeons, park benches, ships. There were also drawings of famous paintings that Ben recognized, and drawings of architectural details so ornate they seemed to be made up or exaggerated.

How could things so ordinary—pencil and paper—be used to create illusions so astonishing? It was almost magical to Ben what his uncle had done. In comparison, Ben now thought his drawings were amateurish, clunky. And yet, he felt inspired to draw. Maybe an artist was what Ben wanted to be when he grew up, after all—if only he could draw as well as Ian.

"How come you make furniture if you can draw like this?" Ben asked.

"Oh, I like building things best of all. I like working

in three dimensions. And I like the fact that a piece of furniture is humble and functional in an everyday kind of way, but if you're good, it can also be a work of art."

Ben was back to the sketchbooks, completely absorbed. "If I could draw like this . . ." His voice trailed off.

And then: a miracle. In the sketchbook before him was a drawing of branches. Initially Ben thought it was simply a pile of branches, a mound, but then he saw the opening, the door, and he saw the way the branches were woven together deliberately, and he saw the curve that was the roof. A hut. A house. It was a house made of branches.

"What is this?" Ben asked, excitement cracking his voice. "Did you make it?"

"Oh, that," Ian answered, craning his neck to get a better look. "I did build that. Years ago, when I was living in California." Ian turned pages to show a number of drawings of the same house. "At the time, I was working on a series of chairs made from branches. And, one day, I was off in some woods gathering branches I could use, when, on a whim, I decided to try to build a little house. I did it for the heck of it. It was fun to imagine people stumbling upon it by surprise as they hiked through the woods." He seemed to delight in the telling. "I imagined them wondering if someone—

or something—really lived in it. And maybe someone or something eventually *did*. I figured I'd never see it again, so I sketched it."

"Was it hard to make?" asked Ben.

"No, not at all."

"How big was it?"

"Oh, big enough for me to fit inside. I had to duck through the doorway, but I could sit or lie in it comfortably."

Ben had more questions, and he asked them. ("Did you bury the ends of the upright branches in the ground to make it secure? Did you use a shovel? A cutter of some kind? String? Nails? How long did it take?" And most important, "Do you think I could build one?")

"You could build one easily," said Ian. "Why? What's up?"

"Oh, I just have a great idea," Ben replied, encouraged. "Thanks to you."

Ben's heartbeat quickened. He could picture it already, and clearly: a perfect house constructed of branches from the Deeters' tree, a perfect gift for the baby. Kale would have to love it. They would be using the tree, it could be fairly big, it would be a house. They could build it right over the stump, if they wanted to. It would be even better than the original gift. And this was something the baby could actually use someday—a secret place, a hideout. He couldn't wait to tell Lynnie.

"Would it be okay to borrow this sketchbook for a little while?" said Ben softly. "I promise to take good care of it."

"It's the house you're interested in, right?"

"Yeah."

"Then here," said Ian, as he slowly, carefully ripped one of the sketches from the book. "Yours." He handed the piece of paper to Ben.

"Thank you. Thank you very much."

"My pleasure."

"Knock, knock," said Ben's mother in a merry tone, a kindergarten teacher tone. She stood at the studio door, her hand curling around the door frame like a vine. "Private meeting? Or may I come in?"

"Enter," said Ian.

Ben rushed toward her. "Mom, I've got to go to the Deeters'. This is extremely important. Please let me do this, and let me skip dinner if this thing that I need to do—which is a good thing—isn't finished. Trust me. Okay? Please?"

She gave him a look that was impossible for him to read.

"I'm helping them with their gift for the baby," he whispered. *"Okay?"*

"Yes, go," she told him, and reached out to touch his shoulder.

But he was gone.

His feet had wings. In what seemed like both an instant and an hour, Ben was standing on Lynnie's front porch explaining his idea in one long, gaspy run-on sentence. ". . . and it'll really work I think and Kale will forgive us I'm sure and this is a drawing my uncle did and we can use it as a guide," he told her, pushing the paper at her, his hand unsteady. " . . . and if you've got clippers, a shovel, and string, we should take them with us even though Ian built his without anything but branches and we should start right away. . . ."

When he finished speaking, he looked at her, his eyes wide, expectant.

Lynnie, who had already been nodding and smiling for about a minute, said, "It's brilliant! You're brilliant. I'll just tell Grandma, and then we can go to the shed and get what we need."

In another instant/hour, Ben and Lynnie were at the site, out of breath, but ebullient and ready to begin.

There were so many decisions to make. They decided not to build the house over the tree stump, but alongside it, so there would be more room inside. They decided to make the house long enough and wide enough and tall enough so that a few people could fit inside at once, so that Kale and Elka could stand up in it. They decided not to use the string to bind the branches together unless absolutely necessary.

They used the shovel to help with the task of bury-
ing the ends of the first branches in the ground to
form the framework. "It looks like a mini-corral," Lynnie observed when they had finished this part. She
squeezed between two of the branches and pranced
around the center in tight circles.

"You're funny," said Ben, smiling. "I mean, in a
good way," he added quickly.

"I know." Lynnie joined Ben by the pile of apple
branches he was sorting through. "Back to work," she
said.

They worked and worked and worked. They clipped
branches, varying the lengths as needed. Starting at
the bottom, they wove the branches into the framework as best they could. Since some of the wood was
brittle, it occasionally broke, and they had to use the
string to tie the pieces together against the framework.

"This is kind of like weaving a big basket," said
Lynnie. "A big upside-down basket."

The words *upside down* made Ben think of the baby,
and he told Lynnie that the baby was breech and how
Nina was trying to turn the baby. He told her about
the ironing board, too.

Lynnie sat down, resting against the stump, as if
considering this required taking a break. She said, "It
seems like everyone has something going on in their
lives that seems bigger than anything anyone else has

going on in *their* lives. I didn't word that properly, but do you know what I mean?"

"Yeah," said Ben. "I think so."

"Sometimes the world just seems so big and full of problems."

"I guess. But we're solving one."

"True."

Ben realized how thirsty he was and how dirty they had both become. His hands and fingernails were filthy, his pants smudged. Lynnie's knees were so darkened and mottled from kneeling they looked like two small, grimy faces with flattened features. A dusty half moon marked the middle of her shiny forehead. "Do you want to get something to drink, or keep working?" he asked.

"Keep working," said Lynnie, springing up and clapping her hands. "We don't have too much left to do."

The house was rising. From jumbled heaps of branches, they were making order, building something useful and fine. The further the house progressed, the more delight Ben took in its creation, and the less guilt he felt concerning Kale. It's beautiful, he thought. But he didn't want to jinx it by saying so. He wondered if Lynnie was thinking the exact same thing. By the time they had fashioned a skeletal roof, he couldn't contain himself any longer. He stood back and said, "This is so cool!"

"It's beautiful!" said Lynnie.

"Outstanding!" said Ben.

Lynnie: "Magnificent!"

Each continued to try to outdo the other with bigger and better adjectives ("Incredible!" "Stupendous!" "Breathtakingly marvelous!") while, in a final burst of energy, they finished the roof and straightened the doorway and patched holes and embedded two old bricks they found into the ground to serve as a threshold.

And then they stood looking at their creation for a long time.

"Are we done?" asked Lynnie.

"I think so," was Ben's measured response.

"Kale and Elka will be so happy," said Lynnie. "They probably won't want to give it up, they'll like it so much."

"Well," said Ben, "the baby won't be able to use it for a couple of years anyway."

"I bet my grandpa will like it, too," Lynnie remarked. "And Grandma. It commemorates the spot, even though the tree's gone."

The sun cut right through the area where Lynnie was standing, a swath of ginger-colored light. She seemed different to Ben all of a sudden—three-dimensional—as if he were seeing her for the first time. Ben grabbed her hand and pulled her inside the house. She squeezed his hand back, stronger than he expected, and he felt shy. They sat down, legs crossed, facing each other.

"I can't believe we actually made this," said Lynnie.

"I know."

Lynnie had discovered some stray aluminum can tabs hidden among the branches. She had tied them to the roof so they hung down into the interior of the hut. She blew at one, and it twirled and swayed. "Finally I feel better about Kale," she said.

"Me, too," said Ben. He struck one of the tabs lightly with his finger.

Lynnie watched him, watched the quick sharp motion of his finger; watched the path of the silver tab intersect a thin shaft of sunlight, watched the tab sparkle. "Hey," she said, "tomorrow, let's hang all the tabs down from the roof, and let's hang what's left of the paper chains all around on the outside. They'll be the finishing touches."

"Good idea," said Ben.

"Want to have dinner at my house?" asked Lynnie. "My dad eats really late, so there's always food around."

"Sure," said Ben.

"Good."

"I go home the day after tomorrow," Ben said, thinking aloud.

"Don't remind me," said Lynnie. "Let's not even talk about it."

"Let's not even talk at all for a minute," said Ben. He yawned. He felt bone-weary, but exhilarated, too.

He lay down, and Lynnie did the same. They were side by side, on their backs, inches apart, staring up at the pieces of the softening sky through the latticework of the roof. The tabs shivered in a breeze, then stilled like raindrops frozen in midair on their descent. The smell was loamy and thick and almost sweet.

After several minutes had passed, Lynnie said, "This is like nowhere I've ever been before."

Ben agreed. "Nowhere."

Part Five

HOME

13

THE LAST DAY. It was early and cool, and the grass in the orchard was jewel-like on account of the dew when Ben and Lynnie met at the little house. Ben had spotted Lynnie, off to the side, coming over a knoll with a duffel bag slung over her shoulder. He figured that she had transferred the paper chains and silver tabs from the old metal cooler to the bag, but he could tell that the bag had too much heft for things so light. She had to have been carrying something in addition to the decorations.

"Hey, what do you have in there?" Ben called, waving.

"You'll see," Lynnie called back. "And good morning."

At the doorway of the house, Lynnie unzipped the bag to reveal the paper chains, the tabs, and breakfast—two apples, two peaches, two doughnuts wrapped in a cloth napkin, and a big thermos bottle of hot chocolate and two plastic mugs.

"Did you eat already?" Lynnie asked. Her eyes were heavy-lidded, still sleepy.

"No. This is great."

They ate the doughnuts and drank the hot chocolate inside the house, saving the fruit for later. Both were very quiet. Steam curled upward from their mugs, veiling their features and disappearing above their heads.

"You still like it, don't you?" Ben asked, meaning the house. He sipped his chocolate, looking at Lynnie over the rim of his mug.

"Oh, yeah," said Lynnie. "Of course. I'm just sad today. You know." She glanced at her watch. "By this time tomorrow, you'll be on an airplane."

Ben nodded. He would be flying home the next morning on a six o'clock flight. "I guess we'd better get moving. We've got a lot of tabs to tie on."

It took much longer than either had expected, but the effect was amazing. Like a collection of stars or a system of planets, hundreds of tabs hung down from the roof on pieces of yarn that varied in length. Back outside, they repaired some of the paper chains and laced them through branches and draped them over knobs and craggy protrusions of bark. The arrangement of scalloped rows looked like bright icing on a cake.

"Good?" said Ben, lifting his eyebrows and sweeping his arms through the air as if he were presenting a prize on a game show.

"Great," said Lynnie. She applauded silently with just the tips of her fingers. "It *was* a house. Now it's a home."

The sky had changed from orchid to blue. The sun and the temperature were rising.

"Let's get Kale and Elka," said Ben.

Lynnie replaced the mugs and the thermos bottle in the duffel bag and moved it aside. "Are you worried?" she asked.

"You mean about Kale?"

"Yeah."

"Maybe a little," Ben admitted. "But he *has* to love it."

"He has to," repeated Lynnie. She clamped her mouth shut in a determined way, and they were off.

≈　≈

Late the previous night, while Ben was eating dinner at Lynnie's—the two of them alone at the kitchen table—they had come up with a plan. Their idea was to bring Kale to the little house by having him ride in Lynnie's grandmother's garden cart. Lynnie had explained the plan, first to her father and then to her mother, as well as she could without ruining the secret.

"That should be all right," Lynnie's father had said. "But check with Mom."

"Just there and back," Lynnie's mother had said. "And either your father or I will help you get him ready."

It was Lynnie's mother who helped. She packed Kale into the cart as if she were packing a porcelain vase into a box to be mailed across the country. Blankets, pillows, and an afghan held him in place. "Listen to Lynnie and Ben," she told Kale. "No goofing around," she said, her finger under his chin, tilting his head so their eyes connected. "And stay put."

"We don't need another tragedy," Lynnie whispered.

"You already scared us out of our whips once," Elka chirped. She beamed at her brother.

"Ready or not, here we go," said Ben. He and Lynnie pulled the cart together, mindful of holes and bumps and rocks, mindful of how fast they were going.

"You're like Colin in *The Secret Garden*," Lynnie said over her shoulder to Kale, "when Mary and Dickon take him to see the garden in his wheelchair."

"It's a *garden*?" asked Kale, obviously disappointed at the prospect.

"Not a garden," Ben told him. "You'll never guess what it is."

"And don't try," said Lynnie. "Just let it be a surprise."

"I love surprises," said Elka. She was wearing her fake casts again. She would imitate the position of Kale's arm and limp along dramatically until she'd fall behind. Then she'd run to catch up and hobble once more. Sometimes she forgot which leg it was she was supposed to be favoring, and had to stop and think.

Occasionally Ben turned to check on Kale. In addition to his casts and stitches, his unkempt hair—stiff and peaked like meringue—contributed to his pitiful appearance, and yet there was something about the carriage of his head and the fact that he was being pulled in the cart that struck Ben as kingly.

When they were getting close, Lynnie stopped. "Remember that Grandpa chopped the tree down. It looks kind of shocking without it," she warned.

"Grandpa said he was sorry," Elka told Ben.

"I don't get it," Kale said. "Are we going to the tree or to the surprise?"

Lynnie and Ben exchanged a glance. Lynnie considered. "Well, it's sort of the same thing. I mean, we're going to see the surprise, but the tree—what's left of the tree—is . . . Oh, just wait and see."

Kale seemed vaguely dissatisfied with her answer.

Ben said, "I know, why don't you two close your eyes, and keep them closed until we tell you to open them?" He told Elka, "I'll carry you." And he asked Lynnie, "Can you handle the cart alone?"

Lynnie nodded. She shook her finger at her siblings. "No peeking."

Elka burrowed into Ben's neck. "Now, even if I peek, I can't see," she said against his skin.

Ben was taken aback by how light Elka was. Her silky hair was the color of lemonade, even more pale than Lynnie's, and smelled hot from the sun. She fidgeted in his arms like a puppy.

They got closer. Ben saw the house in the distance and smiled to himself.

Closer, closer.

And then Kale made a quick gasping sound. His voice rang out, "I see something! I see something! Faster, Lynnie! Faster, faster, faster!"

"What happened to no peeking?" asked Ben.

"Lost cause," said Lynnie.

Elka twisted around. She squirmed free from Ben's grasp and ran to the house.

Ben helped Lynnie with the cart again, and although they were still cautious, now they glided over the tall grass at a clip. Since Kale was not supposed to leave the cart, they circled the house and parked in front so Kale could see inside.

"Wow!" said Kale. "This is so cool!"

Elka poked her head out of the doorway. "It's a house! A real house! And Kale, our magic silver rings are inside like a ceiling that jiggles." Her smile was radiant, and her eyes widened and remained so, as if they had been permanently propped open. She waggled her head, adding, "Oh!"

Because it was nearer, Kale reached out with his broken arm. He uncurled his fingers and touched the paper chains, examined the branches that formed the doorframe. "How did you do it?" he asked.

"It was Ben's idea," Lynnie told him. "We used branches from the tree, so it's really your old gift, just done up in a new way."

"We did it together," said Ben. "We did it for you guys. It's your gift now."

"You still have to add your nests and that old baby doll," said Lynnie. "Those things will really make it yours."

Kale seemed genuinely awed. He smiled suddenly, engagingly, grabbing Elka's shirt and pulling her close. "Hey," he whispered fiercely, not really whispering at all, "we could still give the baby our nests and the doll and keep *this* for us."

Elka tittered at the thought. "We can't do that."

"I know," said Kale. "But we can use it until the baby's born."

"Told you," Lynnie said to Ben.

Ben gave Lynnie a deliberate, slow smile. "*I* told *you.*"

It didn't matter.

Ben felt a lightness expanding in his chest. He had been waiting to hear Kale say, "I forgive you." But, words or not, he already knew that he was. Forgiven.

≈   ≈

They spent the rest of the day together. Since Lynnie's grandmother was watching Kale anyway, she volunteered to keep an eye on Elka as well, which freed Lynnie to do as she pleased.

They hung out in the orchard—straddling low branches, talking about the impending start of school; lying on the ground in the shade, staring up into the density of fruit and leaves, silent; eating far too many apples and peaches.

"I can help you pack," Lynnie offered at one point, peach juice dripping down her chin.

"I just cram everything into my bag and I'm done," said Ben. He threw an apple core at a big, mossy rock. He hit it perfectly, right in the middle, and wondered if the effort had earned him a wish.

They walked and walked, circling back to the little house to admire their brilliance.

"What are you going to get the baby?" asked Lynnie.

"I don't know." He hadn't given it a moment's thought. "What about you?"

"Baby-sitting coupons. I already made them. It's really a gift for Ian and Nina, but that's the best kind of baby gift——one that's for the parents, too."

They ate lunch at Lynnie's house. They ate dinner at Ian and Nina's.

As dusk settled in, they watched Nina, on the ironing board, trying, once again, to turn the baby. Kneeling, Lynnie leaned toward Nina's belly to say a few words. "Turn around, you little thing," she said kindly. "And after you're born, I'll tell you all about your cousin."

Ben's ears reddened.

And then it was time to walk Lynnie home.

"Take a flashlight," said Ben's mother. "And if you're not back in a half hour, I'll start to panic." She winked at him and said good-bye to Lynnie.

Barely a word was spoken until they reached Lynnie's house. The porch light was on, lending a yellowy cast to everything within its reach. Ben studied Lynnie's face. Would he remember what she looked like?

"Bye," he said, looking into her eyes.

"When do you think you'll come back?" she asked.

"Next summer," he replied. "Or maybe Christmas. Summer, for sure."

"Promise?"

"Promise," he said. He knew she believed him.

"You'll have to visit your only cousin," she said, smiling. "You'll have to."

"Yeah."

She stepped backward toward the door, waited a few seconds, and stepped forward again. "Bye," she whispered.

"Bye," he said, edging closer.

There was a moment of awkward bumbling—a handshake from him and a hug from her mixed together. And one last good-bye.

He turned to leave and decided not to look back. He decided to take a new route to Ian's. The sky was enormous, the stars abundant—a basketball net for the gods. He clicked the flashlight off. He wavered between feeling dwarfed by it all and feeling elevated in some way, part of something grand. When he felt elevated, he ran. As fast as he could. Despite the fact that the darkness obscured the bumpy, unfamiliar ground.

14

NINA STAYED IN BED. She had said her good-byes the
night before at Ben's mother's insistence. And although
Ben liked to rise early, four o'clock was even too early
for him. He moved mechanically through the house—
showering, dressing, pouring a glass of orange juice—
like a bleary-eyed zombie.

Under an endless, dark sky, Ben helped Ian load the
luggage into the car.

"Since we've got a minute alone," said Ian, "I just
wanted to thank you again."

"This was a great trip," said Ben.

"If our baby grows up to be half as nice as you,"
said Ian, "we'll be lucky."

Ben extended his hand for his uncle to shake, his
left hand.

Ian squeezed it hard, but not too hard.

"I'm ready," Ben's mother called from the stone
path, interrupting them.

"We're off," said Ian brightly.

Ben crept into the back seat and fell asleep against
the window before the car had reached the highway.
When he woke up, they were coming to a stop in front
of the airport terminal.

The car was in a no-parking zone, so they emptied the trunk quickly while the engine idled.

"I know it was hard for you to ask me to come," Ben's mother said to Ian. Her voice was full of caution and attention. "But I'm glad you did. I'm glad we'll have something to do with each other's lives again. I'm glad you wanted to see me."

"Well—" Ian began. He and Ben exchanged a knowing look. "I'm glad, too." He handed his sister her suitcase, and the visit was over.

Morning was breaking—a smear of rose at the horizon. Less than an hour later, Ben and his mother were boarding their plane, and morning was in full bloom.

≈   ≈

"Are you okay?" asked his mother. She was wrapped in the thin blue blanket one of the flight attendants had found for her.

"Yeah. Why?"

"I don't know. You look—something."

"Just thinking," replied Ben.

"About?"

"Nothing really."

She angled her head and arched her eyebrows in such a way that said: I'm your mother, you can tell me anything.

Ben shrugged.

"I'm sorry you had to see Ian and me fighting the

other night," she told him. "You didn't need to see us act like that." She pulled the blanket tighter around her shoulders, clasping it with her fist at the base of her neck. "I never said I was a perfect mother."

"I didn't either," he said, trying to be funny. But he saw a hurt look cross her face and added quickly, "I'm kidding, Mom. That's called a joke. You're supposed to laugh." He smoothed his kneecaps with both hands.

"I know, I know," she murmured, shaking her head. "Don't pay any attention to me. I'm exhausted." She folded into herself, sinking deeper into the cocoon of the blanket. Soon she was asleep, slumped against Ben's shoulder, her body limp, her mouth open slightly.

Sometimes mothers were difficult to understand. Impossible, even. If she had appeared so wounded because of a stupid joke, he couldn't imagine what would happen if he tried to talk about her being late the day of the accident, or if he told her that it wasn't *her* whom Ian had wanted to see, but *him*. These were secrets, and he would keep them secrets.

The airplane noises pressed into his head. He yawned. He closed his eyes. He thought about everything that had happened in the last few days. How could so many things be packed into so little time? He thought about all the new people in his life. He knew that he would always hold them in some corner of his mind. And he suspected that moments from this trip would rise from his memory at certain times for the rest of his life.

The drift of his thoughts had taken him back to the tree and then in and out of the past several days and back and back to his father and his friends and Gramma Lu and his own house and finally to sleep.

≈   ≈

He woke with an idea. "Mom?"

"Hmm?" She was reading a magazine, the blanket draped over her lap now.

"If I decided not to use my new room as a studio, could I still have it?" he asked warily. "I mean, can I do whatever I want with it?"

She closed her magazine, and fingered the dog-eared cover. "Such as?"

"Well—" He was thinking of changing his tactic. He was thinking that this might not be the best time to spring this on his mother. "Well, I can't tell you yet. I'm still kind of forming my idea."

"Why don't we wait until you've formed your idea," she said coolly. "Then I'll tell you. Fair?"

"Fair," he answered. He would wait. Wait until they were home and his father was present. Wait until she was in an extremely cheerful mood. Wait until the perfect moment.

15

THE ROOM WAS EMPTY, but it wouldn't be much longer. A carpenter would be coming in a few days to start building bookshelves. A sofa—the kind with a bed hidden inside—was on order and would be arriving in a couple of weeks. And soon the nightstand Ben was refinishing would be done. He had found it in the alley behind the bookstore, chipped and dirty, and taken it home to the garage to fix. He had sanded it and given it a thick coat of bright blue paint. What he hadn't done yet, and planned on doing, was to paint an apple on the top and letter the words SEEK NO FURTHER.

The room was to be a guest room. A gift for the new baby. So that Ian and Nina and the baby could visit whenever they wanted.

Ben had told his parents about his idea one night during dinner shortly after the Oregon trip. Ben's father had cooked a fancy meal for no real reason, and everyone had seemed in especially good spirits.

"Let me think about it," his mother had replied calmly. And then no more than five seconds later, she'd said, "Yes," as Ben's father nodded. "I always wanted a guest room."

≈ ≈

Ben's mother had called Oregon, and called again, but there was no change—the baby had not turned. School had begun. One week passed. And another. And the baby's due date crept closer. Ben did his homework at night at the cluttered kitchen table. Most nights now, he could hear both his parents, above him, busy in their studios. His father often paced as he worked, searching for the perfect word, the sound of his footsteps like an animal trapped in the ceiling. And his mother's loom had sprung back to life after lying dormant for so long.

Sometimes, when he had finished his homework, he tried to write to Lynnie, but the words came out all wrong. Sometimes he worked on a letter to the baby, explaining the gift, but how can you write to someone not yet born or named?

So then he would sketch in his book from Ian (in which he safely kept his uncle's picture of the house made of branches). He had been practicing drawing hands. His new art teacher, Mr. McCarthy, said that drawing one's own hands was the best practice for an artist. He said that hands were the most difficult things to draw, and if you could master that, you could draw anything.

Ben mostly drew his left hand, because he was right-handed. Putting down lines lightly at first, setting boundaries, building the form. It *was* hard to do. It *was* hard to get a hand to look like a hand and not some weird sea creature or a row of sausages. When his drawing was going well, he often worked until his mother had to turn off the kitchen light and steer him toward his room. On those nights, he knew, the way he knew his name, that he truly was an artist.

≈   ≈

One evening, after dinner, the telephone rang.

Ben answered it in the kitchen. The voice on the other end was familiar, but shaky. "You're a cousin!" the voice announced, delirious.

And in the instant before Ben even thought to ask, "Is it a boy or a girl?" or to call his parents, or to say, "Congratulations!" he lifted his eyes to the ceiling, to the attic, and he smiled.

Y A

DATE DUE
